THE PERFECT GETAWAY

CHARLOTTE BYRD

CHARLOTTE BYRD
dangerously addictive

Proofreaders:

Julie Deaton, Deaton Author Services, https://www.facebook.com/jdproofs/

Renee Waring, Guardian Proofreading Services, https://www.facebook.com/GuardianProofreadingServices

Savanah Cotton, Cotton's Incision Editing, https://www.facebook.com/Cottons-Incision-Editing-512917856115256/

Cover Design: Charlotte Byrd

Visit my website at www.charlotte-byrd.com

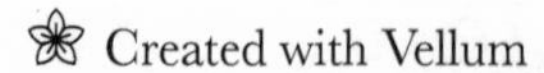

PRAISE FOR CHARLOTTE BYRD

"BEST AUTHOR YET! Charlotte has done it again! There is a reason she is an amazing author and she continues to prove it! I was definitely not disappointed in this series!!" ★★★★★

"LOVE!!! I loved this book and the whole series!!! I just wish it didn't have to end. I am definitely a fan for life!!! ★★★★★

"Extremely captivating, sexy, steamy, intriguing, and intense!" ★★★★★

"Addictive and impossible to put down."

"What a magnificent story from the 1st book through book 6 it never slowed down always surprising the reader in one way or the other. Nicholas and Olive's paths crossed in a most unorthodox way and that's how their story begins it's exhilarating with that nail biting suspense that keeps you riding on the edge the whole series. You'll love it!" ★★★★★

"What is Love Worth. This is a great epic ending to this series. Nicholas and Olive have a deep connection and the mystery surrounding the deaths of the people he is accused of murdering is to be read. Olive is one strong woman with deep convictions. The twists, angst, confusion is all put together to make this worthwhile read."
★★★★★

"Fast-paced romantic suspense filled with twists and turns, danger, betrayal, and so much more."
★★★★★

"Decadent, delicious, & dangerously addictive!" - Amazon Review ★★★★★

"Titillation so masterfully woven, no reader can resist its pull. A MUST-BUY!" - Bobbi Koe, Amazon Review ★★★★★

"Captivating!" - Crystal Jones, Amazon Review
★★★★★

“Sexy, secretive, pulsating chemistry…” - Mrs. K, Amazon Reviewer ★★★★★

“Charlotte Byrd is a brilliant writer. I've read loads and I've laughed and cried. She writes a balanced book with brilliant characters. Well done!” - Amazon Review ★★★★★

“Hot, steamy, and a great storyline.” - Christine Reese ★★★★★

“My oh my....Charlotte has made me a fan for life.” - JJ, Amazon Reviewer ★★★★★

“Wow. Just wow. Charlotte Byrd leaves me speechless and humble… It definitely kept me on the edge of my seat. Once you pick it up, you won't put it down.” - Amazon Review ★★★★★

“ Intrigue, lust, and great characters...what more could you ask for?!” - Dragonfly Lady ★★★★★

WANT TO BE THE FIRST TO KNOW ABOUT MY UPCOMING SALES, NEW RELEASES AND EXCLUSIVE GIVEAWAYS?

Sign up for my newsletter: https://www.subscribepage.com/byrdVIPList

Join my Facebook Group: https://www.facebook.com/groups/276340079439433/

Bonus Points: Follow me on BookBub and Goodreads!

ABOUT CHARLOTTE BYRD

Charlotte Byrd is the bestselling author of romantic suspense novels. She has sold over 1 million books and has been translated into five languages.

She lives near Palm Springs, California with her husband, son, and a toy Australian Shepherd who hates water. Charlotte is addicted to books and Netflix and she loves hot weather and crystal blue water.

Write her here:

charlotte@charlotte-byrd.com

Check out her books here:

www.charlotte-byrd.com

Connect with her here:

www.facebook.com/charlottebyrdbooks

www.instagram.com/charlottebyrdbooks

www.twitter.com/byrdauthor

Sign up for my newsletter: https://www.subscribepage.com/byrdVIPList

Join my Facebook Group: https://www.facebook.com/groups/276340079439433/

Bonus Points: Follow me on BookBub and Goodreads!

facebook.com/charlottebyrdbooks
twitter.com/byrdauthor
instagram.com/charlottebyrdbooks
bookbub.com/profile/charlotte-byrd

ALSO BY CHARLOTTE BYRD

All books are available at ALL major retailers! If you can't find it, please email me at charlotte@charlotte-byrd.com

The Perfect Stranger Series

The Perfect Stranger

The Perfect Cover

The Perfect Lie

The Perfect Life

The Perfect Getaway

All the Lies Series

All the Lies

All the Secrets

All the Doubts

Tell me Series

Tell Me to Stop

Tell Me to Go

Tell Me to Stay

Tell Me to Run

Tell Me to Fight

Tell Me to Lie

Wedlocked Trilogy

Dangerous Engagement

Lethal Wedding

Fatal Wedding

Tangled Series

Tangled up in Ice

Tangled up in Pain

Tangled up in Lace

Tangled up in Hate

Tangled up in Love

Black Series

Black Edge

Black Rules

Black Bounds

Black Contract

Black Limit

Not into you Duet

Not into you

Still not into you

Lavish Trilogy

Lavish Lies

Lavish Betrayal

Lavish Obsession

Standalone Novels

Dressing Mr. Dalton

Debt

Offer

Unknown

THE PERFECT GETAWAY

Broken hearts do not fully heal. Even if they are mended, fissures remain and over time pressure can split open old wounds.

There was a time when Isabelle and I were solid. There was a time when it was just the two of us against the world. I ignored the cracks beneath the surface.

Now, everything is different.

They are after us and they are not going to give up no matter what. They have more resources, more man-power, more strength.

What do we have?

We used to have each other, but now? I'm no longer certain we have even that.

What happens when the new life we tried to build shatters once and for all?

1

TYLER

I'm not sure where to start. I don't know how all of this happened. She showed up in Seattle and suddenly my whole life changed and got turned upside down.

Of course, this is not just because of her. There are a lot of things in motion leading up to this point but now it feels like everything that I have worked for is starting to disappear once again.

When Isabelle and I are together, it's magic.

I don't mean just physically, but also emotionally. Just being in her presence puts my mind at ease. Even though I probably shouldn't be that way.

It's not fair to compare her to anyone else or to compare anyone else to her, but I can't help myself.

I dated Rachel and it was fine. We had a good time. We had fun.

There just wasn't this invisible force pushing us together and it didn't feel like the world might stop spinning on its axis just because wasn't with me.

I didn't know it at the time, but I suspect that she felt the same way. There's a man in her life who has been an on and off again boyfriend for many years.

It was supposed to be over now and they were just friends, but then I found those text messages and I knew that they had been intimate.

I was angry, of course, but more disappointed in myself. The problem was that I didn't really care. I didn't really care about her and I didn't really care that she was cheating on me.

Why was I making all these plans?

Why was I not even entertaining the possibility of moving in with her or marrying her or building my life with her?

What will be the point of all of that?

What was the point of all that?

I had already been with someone who didn't understand me the way that Isabelle does, so why was I doing that again?

The only way to answer that question is to come to the understanding that I believed that I would never see Isabelle again.

I started a new life, with a new identity. Rachel was a part of all of that. So was the Elliott Marina and Hotel.

I bought this place from Mr. Elliott and I promised him that I would keep running all parts of it together as one company. I would not sell the restaurants to the restaurateurs and I would not sell the hotel to the hoteliers.

That's what his sons wanted to do.

That's what his sons are *trying* to do now.

My ownership of this place is in danger and might be reversed. I have a meeting next week with the judge, my attorney, the Elliott sons, and their attorneys.

They're arguing that their father was not in the right mind to sell me this place. They're arguing that their father was always a man who made all decisions based on financial gain and therefore this decision doesn't make any sense.

My attorney tells me not to worry, but I can see the uncertainty in his eyes. I paid almost $20 million for this place, but it would be worth a lot more if it were sold off for parts.

The hotel needs a whole renovation that's going to cost millions. I was planning on getting a loan against the marina, but my attorney put a stop to all of that.

Rachel knows all of this. After I broke up with her, Isabelle came back into my life and I had no idea that Rachel would walk in on us. She's angry at me.

She's embarrassed and humiliated.

I wish that there were something that I could do to change any of this, but I know that I didn't do anything wrong.

I didn't cheat on her. We were not together. She was the one who cheated on me.

She kicked Isabelle in the back and pushed her down to the ground. I had to physically restrain her and pull her off of her.

I'm tempted to punch her as well, but I keep my hands to myself. I won't put my hands on a woman in anger and Isabelle wouldn't want me to do that.

I have never seen this side of Rachel before. She was always so confident and easy-going.

Then again, she has never wanted anything that she couldn't have.

She has worked hard for a lot of things that she has achieved, but everything has always worked out for her.

Of course, she and Michael have had a tumultuous relationship, but I wasn't there for that.

I fold Rachel's arms into herself and usher her out of the cabin onto the deck of the boat. In order for her to get up safely, she needs to climb off herself, but she continues to protest and yell at me.

I remain calm and collected which seems to just make her more upset.

After throwing out a few more slanderous words in my direction, she collects herself and takes a deep breath.

"Oliver, I'm really sorry. I should not have done that. I don't know what came over me."

I nod, letting out a sigh of relief.

Finally, she is calming down.

Finally, she's going to actually get off this boat and leave us alone.

"It's okay," I say. "You were angry."

"I just can't believe what I saw. You two together? At least when Michael cheated on me, I never had to see it."

I can't tell if she's baiting me, but I can't let it go by without correcting her either.

"You know that I wasn't cheating on you, Rachel. We broke up. It's over. I can sleep with whomever I want."

"You wanted to sleep with her?"

"Yes, I did."

"Who is she? How did you meet her?"

"That's really none of your business," I say, shaking my head.

"Yes, it is," she says, her voice going up a little bit.

She's getting desperate again and from this desperation there will be a spark of anger.

I have to stop it, but I don't know how.

She shifts her weight from one side to the other, folding her arms across her chest. She looks tired and worn out, exhausted really.

"I really thought that we had something," Rachel says, taking a step closer to me. "I thought that what we had was really special."

"Is that why you were sleeping with your ex-boyfriend behind my back?"

She raises her hand and slaps me across the face. It burns like hell, but I don't raise mine to her.

"Get the fuck off my boat," I say sternly.

"I don't want to be on this boat," she yells in my face. "I deserve so much better than you, you egotistical asshole."

"I'm not going to argue with that," I say, ushering her closer to the handrail.

I have my hand out to help her jump off, but she does it all on her own.

A wave of relief washes over me. She's safe on the dock and in all of this commotion she didn't end up in the water.

In the little time that I have been living here, I have already seen two people stumble around and end up under the dock as the result of an argument.

"You're going to pay for this," Rachel says, throwing her finger out in front of her and pointing it at me. "You're going to regret ever doing this to me. Who the hell do you think you are? Well, I'm going to find out and I'm going to make you pay."

THOSE WORDS HANG over me as if they are a bubble in a cartoon. I know that is just an empty threat and she doesn't know anything about who I really am, but I know how close she is to the truth.

The thing is that it's not just my past that I'm worried about. It's also the future. She knows about my conflict with the Elliott family. I told her all of the details before I found out that she was cheating on me.

Is that what she means by revenge? Is that what she will do to make me pay for breaking her heart?

When I get back inside, the rain intensifies and Isabelle is trying to dry the clothes that she was wearing earlier in the day.

It has been hours since we met on that bench but hanging all the time in the bathroom has not depleted much of the dampness.

"How are you?" I ask, standing in the doorway. "How's your back?"

"I'm fine," she says, but by the tone of her voice, I can tell that this is not exactly a scene that she wanted to be involved in.

I try to put my hand around her waist, but she pushes me away.

"Why didn't you tell me that you have a girlfriend?"

"Because it's not true," I say. "I caught her cheating on me. I saw the messages a few days ago. We broke up that night."

"She doesn't seem to think so."

"I'm telling you the truth Isabelle. I told her that it was over."

She shakes her head and tries to squeeze some more of the water out of her shirt.

"I just wonder what you would have said if she hadn't cheated on you. Would you tell me then?"

"Yes," I say quickly. It's not a lie or even an exaggeration.

"I'm not so sure," she says with a shrug.

"I know that you don't want to believe me, but I would never do that to you or to her. I'm an honest person."

She turns her head toward me.

"Really?" she asked skeptically.

"Okay, aside from this whole identity situation, I'm an honest person. I would never lie about having a girlfriend if I still had one. No matter how much I might have wanted you."

She shakes her head and continues to face the mirror. I see her hair fall in her face and the tiredness around her eyes.

“I guess this will have to do,” she says, pulling at her clothes.

They are nowhere near dry, but I don't have a dryer nor even a hairdryer here. “This is going to be fine. It's raining anyway. I'm bound to get wet again.”

“You’re not staying?” I ask.

She shakes her head, but I can tell that she is hesitating.

“Don't leave,” I say, walking over and wrapping my arm around her waist.

She starts to protest but I hold her tighter and after a moment she lets go.

When I spin her around to face me, I can tell that there are tears in her eyes.

“You are crying. Why?”

“I don't know,” she says, wiping a tear. “This whole thing has just been very overwhelming.”

“Why don’t we relax? Let's order some food and just hang out.”

I watch her consider the proposal and I hope that she says yes.

After a long pause, she finally nods.

She walks back into the main cabin and climbs behind the dining room table. She pulls her knees up to her chest and grabs her bag, pulling out her phone.

“What do you want?” I ask.

She shakes her head and says, “I don't want to make any decisions right now. I just want to space out for a little bit. Can you just decide for me?”

I nod, understanding.

She has been through a lot.

She just got on the plane last night and now she's here in my arms and in my home.

After I order some Thai food, I take a seat on the couch across from her and close my eyes. I enjoy the silence with her in the same room. It's relaxing and utterly peaceful.

Suddenly, I don't have the need to talk to fill the air with pleasantries. I regret the fact that I never told her about Rachel, but the truth was that there was no time.

I was angry at her. We got into a fight. Then we kissed and did everything else that happened afterward, then we slept and did it all over again.

Perhaps I should've told her more about myself, but it didn't feel right. Actually, I don't think about Rachel at all. I broke up with her that night and we were done. I thought that she was on board for that. In fact, I thought that she was relieved. At least now she can go be with her ex-boyfriend again.

I guess not, though. Rachel can do a lot of damage to me simply by lying. She knows the truth about this place and she knows that I never tricked Mr. Elliott into selling it to me, but that doesn't mean that she wouldn't testify against me if she were angry enough.

I wonder if I should try to see her again to try to smooth things over or would that just make it worse?

When the food arrives, Isabelle and I eat together, devouring it and not saying much. After both of our bellies are full and we feel satiated, she finally looks up at me and says that she believes me.

"I hope that this is not a mistake," she says. "I hope that you're not just misleading me about what happened between you two."

"I'm not. I would never do that. I have never cheated on anyone and I will never cheat on anyone. That's the coward's way out."

"So, if you ever not want to be with me, you'll tell me?"

"Yes, I'll tell you everything. I promise."

We talk a lot over the next few hours. I asked her what she has been up to and about her work.

She tells me about getting fired and starting her own business teaching little kids how to talk. Her whole face lights up when she talks about them and I know how much she enjoys her work.

"This little boy, Loki," she says, "he finally managed to round his lips like this and make an O sound last week. I was so happy."

"How did you actually do it?"

"What do you mean?"

"I mean, how can you make him make that sound if his mom can't?"

"I don't know. It works better with a stranger, to some degree, but I also know how to manipulate his toys. He likes trucks so I hold one that he wants and he has to ask me for it. Then he has to make some sounds. I praise him afterward, but that's how we make progress. A little bit at each session goes a long way. He's making incredible progress."

"I'm really proud of you," I say, sitting back at the dining room table.

"You are? Why?"

"I'm just proud of the fact that you picked yourself up like that and started your own practice."

"It wasn't exactly easy," she says, tossing her hair from one shoulder to another.

"Nothing worth doing really is."

She raises one eyebrow, looks at me, and says, "You know, people say that, but I'm not sure that's exactly true."

"You don't think so?" I ask.

"Nope," she shakes her head. "There are lots of things that're fun to do and that's what makes it worth doing. It doesn't have to be hard."

I tilt my head to one side and prop it up with my hand. A smile forms at the corner of my lips.

"Okay, you got me there. Are we playing semantics here?"

"I just think that it's good to be precise, especially when making blanket statements."

I laugh.

"You get it, right? Being precise with blanket statements, not exactly possible."

"Yes, I get it," I say, nodding my head with great exaggeration.

"I like talking to you," she says after a long pause. "It's so easy and comfortable."

"I agree. I like talking to you too."

After that, we sit for a long time staring into each other's eyes without saying a word. The irony of that situation isn't lost on either of us, and yet the trance can't be broken.

"How long are you in Seattle?" I ask.

"Just a couple of days. Long weekend. I have a flight out on Monday."

It's Friday now. Not counting today, that gives us two full days. That's two days short of the lifetime that I want to spend with her.

"Can we not talk about it?" she asks.

"What?"

"I know that I'm leaving soon and I know that our reunion was a lot better than I ever thought that it would be. I couldn't even imagine it being this magnificent, but I'm leaving and I'm leaving to go back to my new life. I don't want to talk about that now. I don't want to talk about us being apart or what our future holds. I just want to enjoy our time together."

I nod and agree to those terms even though on the inside I am screaming. I want to talk about the future and what's going to happen on Monday because I can't not have her in my life anymore.

This year has been excruciatingly painful. I stayed busy, I worked too much, and the days slipped by, but I wasn't exactly living. I don't want to go back to that.

I want to make a plan. I want to have something to look forward to. Even if she does go back home, I want to know when she will come back.

"What do you want to do while you're here?" I ask as casually as possible.

She smiles and looks out somewhere into the distance.

"I want you to show me around your marina and hotel. I want to visit the Space Needle and I want to sail around on this boat."

"Anything else?"

"Hmmm," she says with a coy smile, tapping her finger on her chin.

"I wouldn't mind going to that famous Fish Market where they throw fish at people."

"That's the same place."

"Can we go to the first Starbucks?"

"Yes, I think so, but I don't know where it is."

"Well, you just have to find out because I've never been here and I want to see it all… with you."

"I like that," I say, giving her a big smile.

Reaching over, I intertwine my fingers with hers. She squeezes my hand and I squeeze back.

"This is going to be our first official date," she says.

"What about all that stuff that happened at your house and our road trip together?"

"It happened, but that was when you were Tyler McDermott. Now you're Oliver Beckett and I've never been on a date with Oliver before."

2

ISABELLE

After finding out about Rachel in that unfortunate way, I tried to get over it and not give it much thought. I believe Tyler when he tells me that they had broken up, not just because I want to but because he also said the same thing to her when she first walked in on us.

She has made a lot of threats that I know are weighing heavily on Tyler's mind, but I don't want to spend the weekend worrying about the future.

Worrying has never gotten anyone anything and though sometimes it's inevitable, for now, I'm going to try to put it out of my mind.

That's why I suggest that we go on a date. Now that Tyler is Oliver Beckett we can be in public and be normal people again. I want to go out.

When we were first together, life was nothing like this.

We were always in hiding.

We were always on the run.

Tempers elevated, consumed with worry.

I want to know what it would be like to actually just be with him. Just the two of us, a regular couple spending a weekend together.

I want to go on a walk.

I want to go to a restaurant.

I want to go to the shops.

I want to do everything that normal people do.

I love Starbucks and, of course, I want to visit the location of the first store. It's located in the famous Pike Place Market right on the waterfront where they toss the fish around in that demonstrative way.

Last night, Tyler drove me over to my hotel and I packed my suitcase and moved to his boat. We woke up around eight and arrived at the market by nine. The first thing I noticed is the modest 45-year-old sign, which only resembles the green mermaid logo that they're using today. It's a sketch of what the logo would become later on and the thing that strikes me the most is not how weathered it looks, but rather how brown.

The rich smell of coffee permeates outside as we get into the long line that curves around the side. The people around us are all tourists like me, making a pilgrimage to a place that has defined their lives.

Perhaps it's an exaggeration to say that a coffee chain defines one's life but for those of us who are fans, I can't imagine going more than a few days without visiting the establishment.

It's this place I think about when I remember studying late into the night in college.

It's this place I think about when I remember awkward dates and fun ones.

"Told you there would be a lot of people here," Tyler says, looking a little bit annoyed.

"Are you worried about… that?" I ask, dropping my voice while I say the last word, suddenly realizing that being in a crowded place all clumped up together is probably not a great idea for an escaped convict.

Tyler pulls his hat down more over his eyes and pops his collar. It's drizzling again and, looking around, I see that he looks like every other guy here.

Bored and in need of caffeine.

"It's not that," Tyler shrugs. "It's just that there's probably another Starbucks two streets over, so why bother with this line?"

I smile, shaking my head. I exchange a significant glance with the woman behind us and she also shakes her head.

"It's not about just having a cup of coffee. It's the fact that this is the place where it all began."

"This isn't the first Starbucks. This is the place they moved to in 1971. The first one was on Western Avenue," Tyler reads off his phone. "But that one isn't around anymore."

"This is the first one that stuck around," I point out. "This one hasn't changed since then. "

"You realize that this is a chain, right?" he asks. "It's one thing to go to some ancient site where a battle was fought and stand on the ground and imagine what it would have been like, but this is a store."

I know that he is joking, except that he's also not.

"You just don't get it," I say.

"No, I don't. Explain it to me."

I take a deep breath.

"Okay, there may be more than 20,000 locations around the world, but this is the beginning of it all. Yes, it's not the only one, but that's what's so special about it. You can go anywhere in the world, almost, and remember what it was like that one time you spent hours studying for a test at one or just got away from a busy day at work and read a good book while drinking a good cup of coffee."

As the long line inches its way to the entrance, I glance to the glass, the floors, the fixtures, and the counters.

Everything here is one-of-a-kind.

The sign at the top of the awning has the name and crude topography, placing one letter in each window. Even the glass looks original and untouched. Inside, a friendly barista takes my order and I can't help but add a mug for souvenir.

Everything about the place puts me at ease, except for the crowd of course.

There are comfortable tables and chairs, weathered only slightly by the passage of time. The colors of the interior are soothing tones of caramel and dark chocolate.

The signage of the bar is made from recycled slate from a local high school and the leather on the bars was scrap from shoe and automobile factories. Even the walnut used on the tabletops and bartop were salvaged from a nearby farm.

When the barista hands me my drink, I ask her about the wall tapestry and she tells me that it has been repurposed from burlap coffee bags from the local roasting plant.

"See, you think that this place is just a chain, without character or any defining features, but it's actually not true," I say to Tyler.

We look around for a place to sit, but it's too crowded and cramped so I suggest that we take our drinks outside and walk around the market instead.

"I was just joking with you, you know that right?" Tyler says.

"Of course," I shrug.

"I mean, I'm not saying that I'm a big fan of huge corporate conglomerates, but I know that you have a personal connection to that place and I should've been more sensitive."

I nod, silently appreciating the gesture. Tyler points me to one of the entrances to the public market, a place that has been an establishment here in Seattle for over 100 years.

"Has it really been here that long?" I ask. "That's a lifetime given the fact that this is on the west coast."

"Yup," Tyler nods. "Pike Place is quite an institution."

I have always enjoyed farmers markets and most of them are outside on an airy street with the vendors lined up down the middle.

This one is more of a permanent establishment with an enormous public red neon sign that reads *'Public Market Center'* and a clock with the time.

The street is wide, made of cobblestones with no parking spots all around, and the market itself consists of shops all along the sides and then inside and throughout.

It reminds me a lot of the Strip District back home. Despite the unbecoming name, it's actually a thriving marketplace of seasonal fruit and vegetable stands as well as flowers and upscale cheese shops.

When I was growing up, it was really the place to go to get affordable fruits and vegetables that you can get at the grocery stores and where my mom liked to shop when sober when she embraced organic eating and other healthy habits.

Since then, it has gone through quite a lot of revitalization with many coffee shops and more upscale stores opening along with the farmers market.

Tyler pops into a flower shop and comes out with a bouquet of sunflowers and daisies.

"Thank you so much," I say, inhaling their sweet aroma. "These are beautiful. Thank you."

I keep breathing in the flowers as we wander around the market popping into a few stores here and there. I'm drawn to one that sells ceramics and I decide to splurge on a big bowl with an elaborate glaze.

"Let me get that," Tyler says.

"No, it's fine," I say, reaching for my wallet, but he refuses to take no for an answer.

"I'd really like to buy this for you," he says. "Is that okay?"

His eyes sparkle as he says that and I can't say no. That's the thing about him, he just has to give me a smile and I find it difficult to fight him on anything.

As he buys me the bowl and I watch the man at the counter carefully pack it in recyclable paper, I wonder what's going to happen in the future.

Where will we find ourselves?

How will this ever work?

What happens when we separate again?

As soon as that last thought occurs to me, I feel a string of emotion somewhere deep inside. It's almost as if I'm made out of strings and that one thought activates and strums one. The sound reverberates like a wave throughout my body and it's all I can do to turn away from Tyler and wipe the tears off my face as soon as it appears.

"Here you go, miss," Tyler says, holding the gift bag out for me. "I can carry it for you if you want. It's a little bit heavy."

"As you wish," I say, looking at him from across my shoulder.

I turn forward and wipe another tear, hoping that he doesn't spot this one either.

AFTER WANDERING around the farmers market all morning, we build up an appetite and head to the restaurant on top of the Space Needle for lunch. The Space Needle is even more beautiful than I had imagined. You take an elevator all the way to the top and then you basically walk out onto glass.

The view is magnificent and the glass floor and the glass walls make you feel like you are suspended in midair. A few birds fly by and for moment I see what they see and I feel what they feel.

"This is a little bit scary," I say, carefully looking down at the floor making sure that my feet are stable.

"I know, it's amazing," Tyler says, jumping up.

He lands silently, but still scares the group of tourists next to us and one woman has to go back inside.

"Sorry about that. Didn't mean to freak you out. Are you okay?"

"I would be lying if I didn't say that this is a little bit unnerving."

"You said you wanted to come here."

"I know, I wanted to look at the view. I'm just not sure I wanted to look at the view through my ankles."

Tyler gets down on the ground and peeks at the buildings and cars on the streets below.

"It's pretty spectacular from here," he says, looking up.

"Get up," I whisper and pull him back up.

I like looking at the water from up top.

It's peaceful and calming. It's nice to sit right next to it and watch the outline of each particular wave, but from here it just sort of washes over me all at once. It's the source of life and it's the source of death, but from up here it's just an ocean of blue.

I look at the skyline for a long time, practically pressing myself against the window.

Tyler stands behind me holding me firmly and occasionally squeezing my hand. When it gets a little more crowded and a little colder, we make our way toward the restaurant.

They seat us next to the window. The restaurant is beautiful and upscale with no expenses spared. I drape my jacket over the back of my chair and order the Forget me Not cocktail: tequila with a garnish of an orange slice and blueberries. Tyler opts for a glass of whiskey and we intertwine our fingers over the table until our drinks arrive.

"You know, I thought this place would be very touristy," Tyler says. "It's actually quite beautiful."

"You know being touristy always gets a bad rap, but what are you supposed to do when you want to visit a place not from there? It's not like locals go out of their way to visit the landmarks that much."

"You have a point," he says, raising one eyebrow.

I'm about to say something else to elaborate on the idea when he raises his glass and says that he wants to propose a toast.

"Thank you for finding me. Thank you for coming back into my life. Thank you for not giving up on me. On us. I know that we're not supposed to dwell on what is going to happen on Monday. I need your promise and my intent is to stick to it, but I just want you to know that I love you. Always have, always will."

I nod and whisper, "Thank you," squeezing his hand.

A small tear runs down my cheek, but I quickly whisked away. For some reason, the toast makes me feel like something else is coming.

A proposal maybe?

It doesn't though.

This isn't a good place to propose, not when you're Tyler. This would be too public and it would draw too much attention to us. I know that and I'm glad that he didn't do it.

Yet a part of me is… disappointed.

Of course, we've never talked about marriage. We had talked about making a life together but not getting married.

Was that implied?

I look up at him and try to think of something to say. It's not that we don't have anything to talk about, it's just that there's only one thing on my mind.

"Are you okay?"

"Yes. I'm good," I say.

"Are you sure?" he presses.

I don't know how to respond. I just stare into his eyes and then break down.

"What's wrong?"

Somewhere in the distance, I see our waiter make his way down the tables toward us. I feel like such a fool.

I wipe my tears away as quickly as I can to try to hide the fact that I am crying. Finally, I give up and just pop on my shades.

I wore them earlier today when it was sunny for that brief thirty minute stretch, but other than that they have been pretty useless this whole trip.

Until now.

“I'm sorry,” I say after my heartbeat slows down and the tequila starts to course through my veins. “I didn't mean to get so emotional. You just said such wonderful things and I want you to know that I love you too. You mean so much to me and I never want to lose you again.”

“You won't,” he says, shaking his head.

I shrug.

“I know that we’re not supposed to talk about this–”

“I can't think of anything else,” I interrupt him.

The waiter comes over and we order food. He lights a small candle and leaves us alone again, surrounded by strangers.

“What's going to happen on Monday?” I ask. “I have to go back. I finally have some work again. I have my mortgage and my other bills. I can't get behind again.”

“I'm not asking you to stay,” Tyler says, intertwining his fingers with mine. “I want to be with you. I want us to be together, but I don't know how.”

“I don't know how either.”

“I can't leave. I have my court case with the Elliott family. I might have to testify. I need to find out what's going to happen.”

“I know,” I say, nodding.

“That doesn't mean that we can't be together,” he says.

“What are you talking about?”

“Just because you're in Pittsburgh and I'm in Seattle doesn't mean that we have to be apart. We can video chat, text, and call. We can arrange to meet up again in a few weeks, after things are more settled here."

"Will you come visit me?" I ask.

"That's a bit complicated, but I'll try."

"Why? What do you mean?"

"Flying is not a good idea for me," his voice drops down a few octaves and becomes barely audible. "I have a new identity and all the legal identifications, but the TSA and all of the recordings of everyone coming, going, that's not exactly the place that I want to be in case anyone is watching."

"Yes, of course," I say, nodding. "I understand."

"I can fly you out. You just tell me when and you'll have the tickets. If you want to stay now, I can help you cover some of your bills."

"No, no, no," I say, shaking my head. "Not that that's not a great offer, but I just can't do that right now. I just started to build up my practice and my students need me."

He nods like he understands, but the thing that I can't tell him is that I have already rebuilt my life once because of him and I don't know if I can do it again.

Nor do I really want to.

If we're going to start something, we're going to do this right. We're going to have a plan and work on knowing for sure that this decision will be forever.

After the food arrives, it smells so good that we both dive right in and push the conversation to the wayside.

With our bellies full and our minds a little bit tipsy, we talk about something else and instead of crying, I start to laugh.

3

TYLER

After lunch at the restaurant, we go to walk along the waterfront. The sun peeks out for only a moment and then hides behind massive clouds once again.

“I like it here,” Isabelle says. “It reminds me a lot of Pittsburgh, but in a good way. It’s newer.”

I hold her hand as we walk past an elderly couple sitting on the bench looking out at the water. They have a small yuppie dog that bounces around them and the man adjusts the dogs raincoat.

“What made you come here?” Isabelle asks.

“I don't know,” I say, thinking back to that scary time when I took off without her and just kept driving north. “I drove for a while and then I saw the sign for the Canadian border. I figured that I should either go back to Seattle or turn right and go back east.”

“What about Canada?”

“I thought about that, but I didn't have identification, not good enough for another country. Plus, I don't know anyone up there. Not that I know anyone down here.”

“What do you mean?”

“Well, that's the thing about starting a new life. It just sort of begins and you have to say goodbye to everyone else that knew you.”

“So, you are not in touch with anyone?”

“Nope,” I say, leaning over the railing and looking at the gray water rolling softly below. “It's kind of the point of getting a new identity. No one is supposed to know who you are now.”

“I like reading about missing people,” Isabelle says.

I turn to face her, not sure exactly what she's getting at.

"I know that sounds a little odd, but they have these shows on television like this. There're also a lot of true crime blogs and websites devoted to missing people. I like stories like that. Not that I am not sympathetic or anything like that, I just like thinking about where they might be."

"I didn't know that," I say.

"I know, that's why I'm telling you now," she says, shrugging her shoulders.

Something changes about her. It's almost as if the cloud covers her and suddenly her mood is darker and more detached.

"A lot of the stories are similar," Isabelle says. "This person is leading a normal life and then he or she disappears. One woman went on a run and left her keys in her car along with a to do list. One man said that he was going to be reporting to his National Guard duty, but instead he went on a long hike a thousand miles away in western Montana never to be heard from again."

"What do you think happened to them?" I ask.

"The woman was never found, but there is some evidence that the Grand Basin serial killer might have killed her because he killed a few other people in the area around the same time."

"And the military guy?"

"A few years later, they found his body. Hypothermia. He was a week's hike away from civilization and there was an early winter blizzard in September."

"Why do you read about these stories?" I ask her.

"I don't know. I guess it's the same reason that people like to read thrillers and watch horror movies. It's scary, but still I'm drawn to it."

"I think there's something else to it," I say.

She turns her face and looks at me. She sighs deeply.

"I guess I felt a little bit like the family members and friends of some of these missing persons. I kept looking for you, but I couldn't find you. It was also worse than that. I couldn't reach out to the police or any authorities because no one could know that I knew you."

"I'm really sorry," Tyler says. "I didn't want to leave alone. You know that. I wanted to go with you."

"I know. It was all my fault. I'm just so relieved now and then I think about what all those other people are going through still living in this waiting room of uncertainty."

I take her hand in mine and pull her closer to me. I kiss her on top of her head, then on her forehead, and then her cheek.

By the time my lips find hers, the dark cloud lifts. She kisses me back and smiles just like she did before.

"Hey, I just realized that I never saw the people throwing fish," Isabelle announces all of a sudden.

"Oh yes, of course! Well, it's back at Pike's Market where we were earlier. Should we head back?"

"No," she says, shaking her head. "Maybe tomorrow."

"I wouldn't want you to miss any sightseeing things that you have on your bucket list."

"Well, I don't plan on this being my only trip to Seattle," she looks up at me and winks.

I smile.

We haven't officially discussed it. We barely just mentioned it during lunch, but I'm glad that this relationship or whatever this is that's going on between us isn't going to be over on Monday.

I told her that it would be difficult for me to fly out to Pittsburgh, but I could easily pay for tickets for her to come to visit me.

Of course, I want her to stay here and live with me, but I also know that she has a life there. I had asked her to abandon it once and to some degree she was willing to do that, but not now.

I know that she's trying to be careful. I know that she's trying to keep her guard up because this past year was as difficult for her as it was for me.

We haven't talked about that either, but I can tell by how she is with me. It's like we are both treating each other as if we were some sort of fragile glass vases that could shatter at the slightest provocation.

After we walk along the waterfront for close to an hour, Isabelle asks to go back to the boat.

"I'm getting a little cold and I'd love to snuggle up by the fire."

"That sounds perfect," I say, licking my lips at the prospect of getting her naked, wrapping her up in a fluffy blanket, and turning on the fireplace.

It's one of my favorite features of the boat. It makes it feel like an actual home and I have spent many nights sitting there curled up with a good book as well as a few bad ones.

We get a cab over to the marina and walk up to the sailboat section on the far end. There by the locked door that leads to the actual boats, I see Tim, my old general manager.

"Oliver!" Tim yells and my back immediately straightens up and my shoulders tense.

As I approach him, I see that he is dressed in a suit with a tie and holding an elegant umbrella over his head to keep himself dry.

His outfit looks like it has been recently dry cleaned and he is as put together as I have ever seen him.

He even got a haircut.

"Hi Tim," I say, walking up to him.

He smiles at me in that unfamiliar way that I have never seen before. I have a feeling that he wants something but that it might take him a bit to ask for it.

“How are you?” he asks. “Hi, I'm Tim.” He extends his hand to Isabelle.

I introduce them, avoiding both of their last names. Luckily, the drizzle stops and I don't feel like I have to invite him onto the boat.

After a little bit of small talk, I ask him what he's doing here. He shifts his weight from one side to another and I can tell that he's a little bit uncomfortable talking in front of Isabelle.

I give her the keys and tell her that I'll be there in a few minutes.

“Is everything okay?” I ask.

“I'm really sorry about what happened,” Tim says. “I’m such an idiot, but I really needed the money. Of course, that's not an excuse!” He throws his hands up in the air.

“I'm sorry that it happened that way,” I say, being careful not to assign too much blame. “I appreciate you coming here and saying this. It takes a lot of guts. Not everyone would do that in your position.”

"I know that I said some mean things, but I didn't mean any of them. I was just surprised, shocked, and emotional."

It feels good to see Tim in this light. Back when he was working for me, he seemed bored, detached, and not at all involved.

I don't know what's different now, except that for the first time he actually seems like he gives a damn.

"Listen, I'm here to ask for my job back."

I open my mouth to say something, but he keeps talking over me.

"I really want you to think about it. I know that I did a terrible thing, but I was in a bind. I've been behind on my rent for months and they're kicking me out. I don't know if you've ever been evicted, but it's a really scary thing. I don't have any family or many friends here and I can't go back to Oregon."

"I don't know what you want me to say," I say, shaking my head. "I appreciate you being so honest with me, but–"

"Oliver, please. I'll never do it again. I'll never do anything to cross you again."

"Tim, I caught you stealing money from me. I really can't take you back as an employee. You were lucky that I never called the police."

"I know, I know that."

"If I had told the police then they would've arrested you and you would have had to plead guilty and you'd never work in hospitality again."

"I know and I appreciate that," he pleads.

"If you needed the money, you should have just come to me. I could have given you a loan against your salary."

He casts his eyes down to the floor. I immediately feel bad. I want to take it all back.

The fact that I haven't had a general manager has become a little tiresome.

He wasn't very good, but at least he dealt with a lot of the calls that I now get directly to my phone number day and night.

For a moment, I consider giving him another chance. Can I actually do that? I know that this is bad and that it would be a bad sign to show my employees that I took someone back who was caught stealing from me, but wouldn't that also show that I'm someone who is willing to give people a second chance?

"I wish that I could help you, Tim, but I can't," I say after long pause of the deliberation.

"Why?"

"I just can't," I say, shaking my head. "Everyone knows that you were fired for stealing and if I take you back then it will be open season on theft from the hotel. We're barely surviving as it is. I invested all of my money in this place."

Tim nods and then stares into space somewhere behind me. I wait for him to say something, but he just sways from side to side in the wind.

"Are you okay?" I ask.

"Do you know what it took for me to come here?"

I shake my head, no.

"I have been sleeping in my car. The homeless shelters are overcrowded, dangerous, and full of psychos. I can't get another job. I tried, but no one is hiring."

"If you want a recommendation, I will give you one. I'm sure that you can get a job at a coffee shop or another hotel."

"Will you tell them about my theft?"

"I won't unless they ask me directly."

He shakes his head and says, "They will ask you why I am no longer working for you."

"I'm not sure what you want me to say," I say, trying to walk past him, but he puts his arm out and blocks me.

"No one is going to give me a job," he snaps.

"You haven't even tried. You can put my name down or even Mr. Elliott's and I'm sure that he will give you a good recommendation if they call. I promise that I will be as discreet as possible, but I can't lie."

I try to get past him again. The dock is narrow and he's blocking my way to the door.

Suddenly, I realize that I don't have my keys. If I want to get back on the boat, I'll have to call Isabelle to come get me.

He doesn't move and I scrunch myself around him, being extra careful so that I don't fall off the dock.

Then he pushes me.

I fall straight into the water and it engulfs me. It's so cold that I struggle to breathe even when I pop my head out of the water.

All of the muscles in my body tighten, making it laborious to even perform the simplest exercise like turning around while treading water and trying to figure out a way to get out.

There are rocks, boulders, on the far end of the dock, sharp and treacherous. I look back up and see him standing above me, his face blank and despondent.

I reach up and grab onto the dock. My clothes, waterlogged, make me feel ten times heavier. I try to pull up, but my hand slips and I slide back in.

"What are you doing? What happened?" I hear Isabelle's voice somewhere far in the distance.

Her footsteps sound like thunder in the water. She swings the door open and kneels down next to me.

"Give me your hand!" she yells.

A boat pulls up causing a small swell of water. From where I am, it throws me all around as another wave goes over my head.

Suddenly, I start to feel warm. It's the first sign of hypothermia, which in this 57 degree water, can set in in minutes.

This isn't good.

My strength is starting to dwindle. Even treading water is difficult and straining.

I pull off my jacket and Isabelle grabs it from me. I reach up again and pull myself up as much as possible. I try to grab on to as much of the dock as I can because I know that she can't pull me far.

From the corner my eye I see Tim, still just standing there, staring at us.

I'm tempted to ask for help, but I'm afraid he might push me off again instead. After a minute or so of struggling, I finally get out.

"You see," Tim says, "now you know what it's like."

His voice is monotone without an indication of any kind of emotion.

"You did this on purpose!" Isabelle yells.

I rub the back of my arms to try to warm up.

I need to get on the boat.

I need to take off all my clothes and try to warm up, but for a moment, I just stand there and stare at him.

"Why?" I mumble, my teeth chattering.

"So that you would know what it's like. You struggled for a few minutes and I've been doing it for days."

"He's out of his mind," Isabelle says under her breath and unlocks the door.

She pushes me through it. The door locks and we walk a little bit down the dock.

When I get on the boat, I turn around to say something else to Tim, but he's already gone.

4

ISABELLE

I saw Tim push Tyler. He put his hands on him and just did it. It was so sudden that Tyler didn't see it coming. He just fell in the water with a surprised look on his face.

I was watching them from the deck of the boat and I jumped out as soon as I saw him do it.

It wasn't an accident. Tim took a step closer, extended his arms, and pushed him in.

"What are you doing?" I yell running over, but Tim just stands there with a muted expression on his face.

I glance over at him as I reach for Tyler and I'm shocked by how absent he looks. It's like he's here but not.

Tyler's heavy. A lot heavier than I thought he would be. He pulls himself as far out as he can, but his lips are turning blue and I can see that the cold is getting to him.

Walking with Tyler with his arm slung over me back to the boat, he shivers so hard that it shakes the whole dock. I help him onto the boat and down the steps into the cabin.

That's when I start to peel off all of his clothing and turn on the shower.

"No, no, no!" he says, stepping out as soon as the hot water hits his skin. "It's too hot."

I feel it and it's barely lukewarm.

"I can't," he says.

I grab his robe and put it on. I turn on the kettle to make him a tall mug of tea, which he holds for a long time before taking a sip.

Finally, after a little while, he starts to feel better. He even smiles and agrees to take a shower.

"That could have gone better," he jokes and I see that he's back to being his old self now.

"Why did he do that?" I ask.

"I told him that I can't give him his job back."

"He was stealing from you though."

"I know, some people are just really entitled," Tyler says, shaking his head.

"So, you know that he did that on purpose, right?"

"Yeah, I do," Tyler agrees.

I'm not sure what else to say except for that I suddenly notice that my hands are shaking.

"Are you okay?"

"Yeah, I just keep thinking that you could have died."

"Well, that's kind of an exaggeration," Tyler says, shaking his head.

"Is it? That water is freezing. If I hadn't been there, you would not have been able to get out. Then what? Tim didn't look like he was going to help you."

"I would have swam to the rocks."

"The waves would have pummeled you against them."

Neither of us say anything for a little while thinking about that.

If this had happened to anyone else then the right thing to do would be to call the police and to report what he had done, but it didn't happen to anyone else.

It happened to Tyler.

The problem is that we *can't* call the police.

"What are you going to do?" I ask.

"About what?"

"About Tim?"

"I'm really tired, Isabelle I don't know."

He leans back against the couch and closes his eyes. His skin feels warm now and everything is seemingly okay, but I have a nagging feeling that makes me think that it's not and it probably won't be for a long time.

"Do you mind if I just go and lay down for a little bit?" Tyler asks.

"Of course," I say and watch him disappear into the cabin.

I pull out my phone and scroll through social media, looking at nothing in particular. I have a few messages from Libby and I ask about the kids. Neither of us talk about my mom. She doesn't bring it up and I don't either.

Listening to the rain drum steadily outside, I feel my eyelids getting more and more tired. The light in the cabin is off and I carefully tiptoe onto my side of the bed.

Tyler is already asleep. I look at his face, calm and peaceful. He's sleeping on his side, propping up his head with his arm. I close my eyes and slowly drift off.

A little bit later, a loud ring wakes me up. I don't know how much time has passed and it takes me a few minutes to realize that it's coming from Tyler's phone.

He grabs it groggily from under his pillow and answers.

I can tell that it's someone calling from the hotel, but I don't know what's really going on.

Tyler nods his head and sighs a few times, finally saying that he'll be there as soon as he can.

“What's going on?” I ask when he hangs up.

“That was Eileen. I have to go in.”

“Who is Eileen?”

“Manager of housekeeping. She called to say that Tim is there and he's making a scene.”

“You should not go there,” I say.

“I'm the owner. I have to.”

“This isn’t a good idea,” I say, but he's already dressed. “What about what he just did? What if he attacks you again?”

“I can take care of myself.”

“I know that you can, but you're not thinking clearly.”

“What do you want me to do, Isabelle? I have to go.”

I try to reach out to him, but he shrugs me off. I can tell that his mind is elsewhere now.

He is singularly focused on this one problem, but the issue is that there's something much bigger going on here.

It's not that I'm afraid of him getting physically hurt. I know that in hand-to-hand combat, Tyler could easily take him, especially now that he is so much bigger and bulkier.

That's not the problem.

The problem is that if there's going to be a scene then there's going to be a good likelihood that the police will show up. That's the thing that he can't allow to happen.

I sit on the edge of the bed for a little bit and then decide to run after him. I climb the deck of the boat and then jump onto the dock.

I run all the way to the security door, but I see that he's already gone. I don't have a car and if I want to catch up with him, I have to take a cab over there.

I'm not sure what to do. Dressed in only a light T-shirt and pajama pants, I wrap my hands around myself and head back to the boat.

When I get into the cabin, a dark cloud descends over me. I don't know what's going to happen, but it's not going to end well.

I'm not sure if there's anything that I can even do about it.

5

TYLER

When Eileen calls me, I wake up feeling a little woozy and still feel sick to my stomach. The chill down to my bones is gone, but something remains with me about what happened earlier on the dock.

There's a heaviness and I can't push it away. Now, driving to the hotel to face Tim again, I know that it will take a lot to get rid of him.

Isabelle tried to stop me from leaving. I know what she's worried about. It was a mistake *not* to report his theft and it was a mistake not to report him pushing me off the dock, but what choice do I have?

I have a new identity and a new look, but that doesn't mean that an inquisitive police officer with a little bit too much time on his hands won't be able to connect the dots and discover who I really am.

Luckily, Tim doesn't know anything about that.

Right now, he's just angry. He's upset that I caught him stealing and he's mad that I refused to forgive him and give him his old job back.

The fact that I promised to give him a good recommendation for the work that he did do seemed to fall on deaf ears. I don't know if he saw that as weakness but it definitely wasn't.

Kindness is often mistaken for weakness when it is actually the opposite. To be kind in the face of adversity and hatred is something that a weak person can't do. It's only something that a strong person can do.

When I get to the hotel, I leave my car with the valet but tell him to keep it in the front of the lobby.

I look around to make sure that Eileen hasn't called the cops. I texted her not to, but things might have escalated since then. Luckily, I don't see any flashing lights or hear any sirens in the distance.

As I walk into the lobby, I can almost hear Isabelle's voice standing in for my conscience.

"Why can't they just take care of it? You have a security guard, right?"

I know exactly what she's worried about. The same thing that worries me. I can't not go and deal with things.

Tim is making a scene. He has a few drinks in him, more than a few actually, and he's refusing to pay for them.

Hank, the security guard who works nights, is trying to get him out, but he's refusing to go.

"If you want me to leave, you have to call the police," Tim says, slurring his words.

I know Hank is hesitating. He and Tim used to be pretty close, even went fishing a few times.

If he calls the police and Tim keeps fighting and tries to resist them, then there's a chance that they will arrest him for something and that will end his career in hospitality at least as far as general management goes.

“Come on Tim,” Hank says, trying to usher him from his barstool. “Why don't I call you a cab?”

“I don't need a cab,” Tim says slowly but loudly. “I'm going to stay right here and have another drink.”

Tim looks disheveled and tired now. His tie is loose and his suit is wrinkled.

He leans on one hand to prop up his head and his hair looks like it has been through some sort of wind tunnel.

I start to walk toward him, but Eileen pulls me aside. She's a no-nonsense woman in her mid-50s who has been managing housekeeping at the Elliott Hotel for most of her adult life.

She has grown children and two grandchildren who live with her and she does not suffer fools lightly, as the saying goes.

“He's going through a divorce,” she tells me. “That's why he got kicked out of that apartment. His wife moved out and he couldn’t afford the rent. He can't afford to pay for the lawyer and he's worried about losing his kids.”

"What do you want me to do?" I ask. "You want me to take it easy on him?"

"I don't know," she says, shaking her head.

"He came to the boat today and asked me for his job back, but of course I can't do that. I caught him stealing. I told him that I would give him a recommendation, but that wasn't enough."

Eileen nods and points out, "Most people wouldn't even do that."

"I'm not trying to be a bad guy," I say. "I have to look out for this place. I can't have the GM stealing from me."

"Yes, I know."

"Oh, perfect, you're here!" Tim yells out from across the restaurant.

A few people look up and I know that I can't let this go on for any more time. It's Saturday night and the place is busy.

So far, Hank has done a good job at keeping him quiet. Unfortunately, I don't think he'll stay that way now that we are going to have a conversation.

I wave him over, trying to get him away from the bar and all of the patrons into a more private place, but he just shakes his head and continues to nurse his drink.

"I hear you're refusing to leave," I say in a hushed tone into his ear, hoping that no one hears us.

"So what?"

"This is my establishment and these are my employees. If one of them asks you to leave, then you leave."

"What are you going to do about it?"

"I don't know why you're being so difficult, Tim. I know you are going through a hard time right now, but I wasn't the one who was caught stealing. If you need help, I'm willing to help, but so far you have asked me for nothing."

"What are you talking about?" he roars. "I asked you for my job back, remember? Did you forget? Was the water so cold that it erased some of your memory?"

I clench my jaw and form my hand into a fist. Still, I force myself to stay calm.

I can't hurt him.

There are too many people around and if I swing at him, it's going to end badly.

My only goal now is to get him away from here.

"If you want to talk about this, let's talk about it somewhere else. I'm not going to do it here."

I turn around and walk away.

This is incredibly difficult, but it's the only way that I can lead him away.

I turn back to see if he's following me, but he's not.

Shit, I say to myself.

I wait for a few more minutes but he's still at the bar.

Just as I'm about to give up hope, Tim walks over to me.

His body sways from side to side because he is unable to maintain a straight line.

Once, he even leans on a table for support.

Once we are in the hallway and away from the bar in the restaurant, I let out a sigh of relief.

"Okay, this is good," I say to myself. "This is progress."

By the time he reaches me, I can see that he has no plans of leaving. His face is tense and his lips are pursed.

He looks angry.

Upset.

Disappointed. All at the same time.

"I heard that you were going through a divorce," I start to say, but he raises his hand and punches me right in the mouth.

I get dizzy and nearly fall over, but I catch myself on the wall. When I pull my hand away from my mouth, my palm is covered in a dark brown liquid, my blood.

I make a fist to swing at him as well, but I stop myself in midair just as Hank rushes up to us. He overpowers him and throws him down on the floor. I taste lead and iron between my teeth and try to get my head to stop spinning.

"I'm so sorry, boss. Are you okay?" Hank asks over his shoulder, while holding Tim down with his face pressed to the tile.

"I'm fine," I say over and over again. "Just get him out of here."

"I've already called the police."

My blood runs cold.

"You did?"

"Of course. He attacked you."

"Yes, you're right," I stutter. "Of course that's the right thing to do."

Tim stops fighting when he hears that and allows Hank to escort him to his office. I promise to stop by once I get myself cleaned up.

Looking at myself in the mirror, I realize that I'm quite a sight.

Lip split open, blood gushing everywhere. I reach for a paper towel, wet it under the faucet, and bring it to my face. Then I stop.

No, I can't do that. This is the perfect cover.

The messier I look, the harder I will be to recognize.

I step into Hank's office and take a seat across from Tim.

I wait for him to say something, but he doesn't. He just buries his face in his hands.

A few minutes later, a police officer arrives. He pulls me aside, asks me what happened, gets a statement from Hank, and then one from Tim.

"Would you like to press charges?"

"No," I say.

Tim looks up at me surprised.

The cop doesn't seem bothered by it one way or another. It's just something in the day of the life of his job.

He asked Tim to follow him and he does. Tim looks back at me, but only once.

NEITHER HANK nor Eileen are surprised that I don't press charges. They have worked with Tim for many years and have a lot of positive things to say about him.

On other occasions, they told me about all of the good times they had working at this place. They also told me that there was a time when Tim was highly motivated and a great general manager.

Mr. Elliott would not have kept him on this long if he weren't. Before driving back to the boat, I stop by the bathroom again and wipe my face as well as I can. My lip has already gone puffy along with part of my chin and I won't be able to hide this from Isabelle. Not that I want to.

Luckily, the cop was tired and not particularly interested in anything to do with me or the hotel other than taking my statement. I hope that for now that's enough.

I hope that Tim leaving in a police car is enough to teach him a lesson and to leave me alone. I have given him so many chances.

I hope he doesn't waste them. I also hope that he stays away not only for his sake but also for my own.

When I get back on the boat, I realize that I've been gone for hours. I hope that Isabelle is asleep, but when I see her sitting in the cabin curled up in a blanket with that angry look on her face, I know that this is going to be a long night.

6

ISABELLE

I wait for him for a long time. I try to sleep, but I can't. I didn't want him to go back to the hotel tonight, but I know that it's his job and that I don't really have much say in it.

I try to occupy myself by pacing around the cabin and eating almost everything that's in the refrigerator, but none of that calms my nerves.

I don't know why I suddenly feel so on edge. I wanted him to stay because having another interaction with him is probably not the best thing in the world, but what can you do?

When Tyler finally gets back, I see his lip is swollen and I know immediately that it didn't go well.

"Are you okay?" I ask, trying to keep my anger at bay.

"I'm fine. You didn't have to wait up."

"I know, I wanted to. I was worried."

He shrugs and heads straight to the bedroom.

"What happened?"

He brushes his teeth and examines his face.

"He didn't want to leave," he says.

"And?"

He shrugs.

"You got into a fight?"

"I don't want to talk about it," he says.

I nod, trying to understand, but I can't without actually talking about it

"You need to tell me something, Tyler."

"Isabelle, this has been a long day and I need to get some rest." The tone of his voice is short and abrupt. He's dismissive and I don't like it.

I open my mouth to say something else, but then I close it. I know that he needs space and maybe what I need right now should go on the back burner.

He climbs into bed beside me and turns around to face the wall.

I feel frustrated, out of control, and mostly upset. I waited up and worried and now I don't get anything in return. Not an explanation or anything else.

A few hours later I'm still awake, still stirring. Tyler is fast asleep and the fact that we haven't talked about anything is making me more and more upset.

I pull out my iPad and try to read something, but nothing keeps my interest. I put on Netflix, but an hour goes by before I notice that I'm not paying attention.

Eventually, early in the morning, I finally drift off, but the sleep is not peaceful or long.

The morning is gloomy and blue. Clouds are hanging low and the sun cannot penetrate them.

I know that it's out there somewhere, but I haven't seen it the whole time I've been here and it's not exactly helping my mood.

I'm leaving tomorrow.

The thought of that dawns on me just as I stretch my arms over my head. This is our last day together and I'm both grateful and irritated at the same time.

When I first came here, I only partly expected to see him, but then, here he was and things between us were even better than they were before.

What happens now?

I miss him already even though we're not yet apart, but I'm also still upset and angry with him, largely for not talking to me last night and not telling me what was going on.

I know that it's irrational. I should have just slept, but that's the thing about emotions, they are often difficult to control. All you can do is feel them and hope that they rush through you without creating too much damage.

Walking into the kitchen, I see Tyler barefoot as always and dressed in his sweats making a stack of pancakes and a large omelet with finely cut up broccoli, asparagus, bell peppers, and mushrooms.

"I wasn't sure what you wanted," he says, smiling at the corner of his lips.

“Everything,” I say. “I'm famished.”

I take a seat at the table and then realize that there are no plates or utensils. I jump up and grab them from the cupboard next to his head.

“Where did you get all this? I thought that I had eaten everything in your fridge last night.”

“Yes, I’d noticed that,” he says with a smile. “Luckily, there's a market right across the street that opens early.”

“This smells delicious,” I say, taking a whiff from the stove.

“I'm an expert in breakfast foods.”

After setting the plates and the cups, I walk around him to grab the utensils and he stops me. He spins me around and kisses me on the lips.

“What is that for?” I ask.

“It's an apology.”

I avert my eyes, pretending like he has nothing to apologize for, though secretly I really appreciate it.

“Yesterday was a really bad day,” Tyler says. “I mean, it was perfect right until Tim showed up.”

"God, I wish I could have socked him," he says, making his hand into a fist and then forcing it open. "But I'm glad I didn't. It would just have made things worse for me. He might have called the police and pressed charges."

"He wouldn't have been in the right since he did it first."

"Of course, but it would have made the whole thing a lot more complicated. The cops would have a lot more questions."

I nod, getting that familiar feeling in the pit of my stomach again.

"So, you didn't talk to any police officers?"

"I did," he says and my whole body tenses up. "Don't worry, it was fine. Tim bloodied my face so that was a good thing. The cop could barely look at me and didn't take very long to take my statement."

"You're not pressing charges?"

"Of course not. I can't risk testifying against anybody in any court."

I reach over and give him a hug. With my head pressed against his chest, I can hear the pounding of his heart.

It's going fast, faster than normal and I know that this is much more difficult on him than it is on me. It's his life on the line.

"What about the hearing for the hotel sale?"

"Yeah, I don't have much choice about that."

We both sigh at the same time.

"My attorney is going to take care of it. It's before the civil court judge and I just hope that no one looks too closely."

After all of the pancakes are ready, we dig in. I grab a portion of the omelet and a pancake, smothering it in maple syrup.

"This is so good," I say.

"You're just hungry," he jokes. When he tries it, he nods approvingly and agrees, "It is good."

We try to talk about something else, but neither of us can really come up with a good topic. There're only so many times that you can say that it's rainy before you have to move on to something else.

I talk a little bit about my new clients, but it's all the stuff that I have already told him. I don't want to talk about my mother and neither of us want to talk about what's going to happen tomorrow.

Besides, my thoughts keep circling on only one thing.

"I know that you wanted to buy this place because you wanted to stay busy and do something productive and more hands-on than buying and selling stocks, but this place could also be your downfall," I say.

Tyler breaks off a big piece of his pancake and shoves it into his mouth.

"I don't think I'm saying anything that you don't already know."

"You're not," he mumbles, chewing with his mouth closed.

"I'm sorry to bring it up again, but I'm just worried."

He swallows, looks at me, and responds, "I know that you are. So am I."

"You are?"

"Of course," he shrugs. "When I bought this place, I thought it was a clean deal. I knew that the sons didn't approve, but I didn't think that they would push it this far. I didn't think that they would try to take it from me."

"Well, you know how people are when they think that they're entitled to something that they have no right to."

"You have to believe me that Mr. Elliott was of complete sound mind when we made this deal." There's an intensity to Tyler's voice. Even an urgency that I don't really remember hearing before.

"Of course, I believe you. I know that you would never take advantage of him like that."

"It was an honest and fair deal. I probably even paid too much. His wish was that I keep this place altogether. The marina, the hotel, and the two restaurants. Honestly, that's not a really good financial decision. All parts of it are worth more individually than they are all together and yet I intend to keep my word, even if he has no way of forcing me, legally, to do that."

"I'm sorry, Tyler," I say, putting my hand over his from across the table.

"I sometimes think that I should just cave," he says. "Just give them what they want. Avoid the trial and everything that goes along with it."

"And?" I ask, my heart skipping a beat. I don't want to say this out loud yet, but that's not the worst idea.

He doesn't respond.

"How would that work exactly?"

"I could just tell my lawyer that I don't want to fight. There are three of them making a case. In situations like this, the family often wins because judges tend to side with families. It would be one thing if there were one brother pitted against another, but that's not the case. I'm a stranger and it's going to be an uphill battle, not to mention exorbitantly expensive to fight it."

"I'm here for you no matter what you decide to do," I say. "I believe you and I know that Mr. Elliott wanted you to have it, but if he doesn't want his sons to inherit then he should have put that in his will. I agree with you, it doesn't look good."

He nods and looks somewhere far in the distance.

"What about his wife? Their mom?"

"She's not their mom. His current wife is his second wife and I didn't get the sense that she really got along with the sons."

I nod, realizing how complicated it is to have a lot of assets in a big family and grown children fighting for their share.

"You know that your decision here can just be about the truth. You have something bigger to hide and this agreement and legal battle can really expose you. You don't want people after you with an ax to grind."

"Of course not," he says calmly. "That's precisely why I didn't press charges against Tim and why I didn't want to call the police at all. I had to think about the bigger picture. I have to think about... us."

"Us? What about us?"

"Our future. That is if you…"

"Of course," I say, letting a wide smile spread over my face. "I wasn't sure if you had thought about things like that."

“I have, many times. I was actually thinking about proposing to you the last time we were together.”

The words feel like a gust of wind pushing me back.

“Sorry, I didn't mean to startle you,” he says nonchalantly.

“No, not at all,” I say quickly. “I just had… no idea.”

“I know that the thing to do when you're thinking about proposing to someone is to just pop the question, but we haven't known each other long and our relationship is not under the most normal circumstances. So, I just want to ask you straight up.”

“What?” I ask.

I lick my lips and feel how dry they are, my mouth is a complete desert.

“I just want to know whether you ever thought or think that you would, maybe, in the future want to marry me?” His question is convoluted and imprecise, very much unlike him.

“Of course,” I nod my head vigorously.

“Of course?”

"Yes. I don't know if you're really asking me right now or asking me about what might happen in the future, but the answer is yes to both."

"I love you, Isabelle."

"I love you too," I say, pressing my lips to his.

I open my mouth and his tongue finds its way inside. I feel the prickle of his two day old beard with my fingertips as I slide them into his hair.

I want to ask him to clarify. I want to know if that was a proposal or if I should expect one sometime soon, but the harder that he kisses me, the harder it is to pull away and to make words resemble any sort of thoughts.

Our bodies find each other and immediately everything starts to make sense again. He runs his fingers up my spine and buries his hands deep in my hair.

He twirls it around his hand and pulls slightly, sending shivers down my arms. I lose myself in that moment where pleasure borders on pain.

I kiss him harder. So hard that our teeth collide. He pulls away from me and I laugh.

He laughs along with me.

The thing is that it could ruin the moment, but it doesn't. Once our eyes meet something shifts and this time when I reach over to kiss him, it's more delicate and soft.

I run my fingers along his chiseled jaw and toss his strands of hair away from his eyes. He closes his eyes and presses his lips to my ear lobes, purring softly.

"I love you," he whispers and I whisper back to him.

His hands run up to grip my arms and suddenly I become keenly aware of how big I am.

When I look into his eyes, I see nothing but admiration and his lust for me, equating the way that I feel for him.

I press my body closer to him and he runs his mouth down my neck and then over my clavicle. He toys with me as I tilt my head back and enjoy the moment.

His hands find my breasts and I tilt my body away from him, giving him as much leeway as possible.

Tugging at my shirt, he unbuttons it and pulls it over my head. I reach over to take off his but he does it for me. I let my hands run up and down his hard abs, watching them tense and relax with each breath.

He looks up at me, looking almost shy, perhaps uncertain of exactly how attractive he is.

Somehow, when our eyes are locked on each other's, the world just makes sense. Whatever trepidations or uncertainties I have, they also leave.

Tyler takes my hand and pulls me close. Our lips touch again and so do our bodies. We are skin to skin and I've never felt safer or more turned on. I unbuckle his pants and let them drop to the floor. He pulls off mine. In the meantime, we keep our lips touching or as connected as possible.

He lifts me up and carries me over to the bed. I wrap my legs tightly around him and continue to kiss his mouth.

When he plops down, he slides right inside, taking me by surprise. A very nice surprise.

With my arms thrown back, he drapes his strong body over mine. He continues to kiss my mouth and my neck as he thrusts himself deeper inside of me, practically splitting me open.

The familiar, warming sensation starts to build at my core and quickly spreads everywhere. He catches me completely by surprise and I ride the wave until my legs cramp up and I have to curl my toes to make it go away.

"I love you. I love you," I say over and over again.

"I love you, too," he whispers.

7

ISABELLE

Wrapped in the afterglow of what just happened, I pull the sheet up to cover my breasts and then turn to face him.

He props up his head with his arm and twirls a few strands of my hair around his finger.

"If you could be anywhere right now, where would you be?" I ask.

"Right here," he says, leaning over and giving me a kiss.

"No, I mean, me too. Except I was just wondering if you'd preferred to be somewhere a little bit less rainy and gloomy?"

"It could be raining buckets and there could be a -50° wind chill, but as long as you're there, I'm happy."

I roll my eyes and laugh. Clearly, I'm not getting through.

"Yes, me too, of course," I say. "Wouldn't it be nice if we were, say, on this boat but somewhere in California or Hawaii or the Florida Keys or the Caribbean?"

"Because it never rains in Hawaii, the Caribbean, or the Florida Keys?" he asks, his tone drenched in sarcasm.

"Not cold rain," I point out. "You don't need your jacket."

"Yes, I guess. Is that what you want?"

"I'm not the biggest fan of Pennsylvania winters or the fall or the spring for that matter. I heard that the summers here were nicer, but the other nine months? It's a lot of gloomy days."

"Are you talking about a trip or something more permanent?" Tyler asks.

I think about that for a moment.

"Well, in a dream world, it would be nice to make that permanent. Somewhere warm, tropical, beautiful."

"Pacific Northwest has a lot of beauty," Tyler says. "I'd like to show it to you sometime."

"Yes, of course. I'm not saying that it doesn't. I love the fact that it's evergreen here year-round. There're so many trees and it's actually quite wild for how many people live here and all the water."

"There are a lot of whales and sea lions who live around here. I'm sure that you'd like to see them."

"Of course."

I quiet down for a moment. Is this what he means? Is he really planning on staying here forever?

I don't know exactly how to approach the subject without making him feel bad, but it's getting close enough to my departure that I need to have some answers.

"So, how do you think this is going to work?" I ask. "Between us?"

"I thought that you don't want to talk about that."

I shrug, pick at one of my nails, and whisper, "I don't really, but we have to. I want to see that we were on the same page."

"Of course we are. I almost asked you to marry me and you clearly said yes."

I look up at him and he smiles at the corner of his lips.

"What then? I mean we never really talked about it before and now you're here and you own this big business. Would you like me to move here to be with you?"

He sits up in bed and looks straight at me. Then, quickly, he averts his eyes.

"I made the decision to buy this place when you weren't in the picture. You were gone and I never expected to see you again. I did this for me."

"Yes. I know," I say quietly.

I want to add that I know that I messed up, but I don't.

"I don't want to ask you to do something that you don't want to do," Tyler says. "I know that you have a home in Pittsburgh, a mortgage, the new business you're starting, and clients that depend on you."

"Yes, I do have those things, but you have this hotel, this marina, and those two restaurants that you can't leave."

"What are you getting at, Isabelle? Do you want to come here?"

I take a deep breath.

"I want to be with you," I say. "I like what I saw of Seattle so far, but I do know that the weather will get to me. I'm not my best self in the midst of the Pennsylvania winter and though it is green here, it's a lot more gloomy."

"The thing is that I don't know if we have to make a decision right away. I have this whole situation with the court and I don't know what's going to happen to this place. Who knows, perhaps the Elliott brothers will win and I'll have to give it back."

"Don't say that," I shake my head. "You bought it fairly and at a good price for both of you."

"Yeah, I know that, but that doesn't mean that I'll be able to prove that and I have to prepare myself for that fact."

I nod, putting my hand on his shoulder, being as supportive as I can.

"The truth is that it might not be such a bad outcome. I wanted to run this place and I was all alone and was getting tired of just staring into a computer screen day in and day out. I wanted to do this so that I could bury myself in a different kind of work and to stop thinking about you. Now that you are back in my life? I don't know, somehow, working 60, 70, 80 hours a week, if not more, is no longer that appealing."

"Are you serious?" I ask, not exactly believing him. "Please don't say that because you think that this is what I want to hear. I'm really proud of you for getting this place. I know that you can make it work if you are just allowed to make all the changes you wanted to."

"It would be a lie to say that this has nothing to do with you, but things change. Priorities shift."

"It doesn't have to be that way."

"What are you talking about?"

"You could just ask me to move here? It seems to be the most obvious solution."

"What about your house, your business, and the fact that you're not really on board with all of this rainy weather?"

"I know, that's true, but you know me. I'm not a huge fan of Pittsburgh either. I just went back there because my mom was with me and that's where my job and my work are. That doesn't have to be the case. Not if we try to build something together."

"I like that," he says, reaching over and giving me a kiss. "I like the idea of thinking about us starting something together as a couple."

He kisses me again and I kiss him back. I feel the bed calling to us again, but there's something else that I want to do.

"Take me out on your boat," I say.

"I thought you would never ask."

HALF AN HOUR LATER, we stand on the deck with Tyler at the wheel and pull away from the dock. The engine putters along and Tyler expertly maneuvers out of the marina and into the bay.

The wind is strong, slashing against my face, perfect weather for sailing.

I have never been on a sailboat before and I'm not exactly relaxed or warm, but I sit with my arms wrapped firmly around my knees, wishing that I had put on another layer.

Tyler unfurls the mainsail and it quickly fills with wind. Suddenly, we are flying through the water. He turns off the engine and everything becomes silent.

I hear the squawking of the birds overhead, but there's no annoying sound of machinery grinding and working to give us momentum.

When we turn, or what he refers to as tacking, he shows me how he does it and then helps me run the lines myself. I love watching the mainsail and the jib fill up with wind and glide us over the dark water.

Tyler takes us closer to shore so we can see the magnificent contemporary mansions lining the bay. He doesn't know who owns them, but each one costs multiple millions and I suspect that they belong to the heads of companies.

Most of them are blocked with thick vegetation from one another, have enormous docks and boats up front. From the water, you can see straight through all of the glass and deep into each one.

We are one of the few boats out here and it feels serene and peaceful. Tyler steps away from the wheel and I pull out the picnic basket that I packed downstairs.

Unfortunately, it's too windy to enjoy it, even once we put down the sail. We end up just having the drinks and sitting and looking out at the horizon.

We talk about everything and nothing at all and point out that we have similar tastes in music, art, and movies. He's even seen the more obscure indie flicks that I tend to like.

After a little while, the clouds come in and the slow drizzle turns into thick drops of water. There isn't much shelter and we decide to head back.

"Why don't you go downstairs after I put the sail up so you don't get soaked," Tyler says.

I nod and help him with what I can, even though he clearly doesn't need my help.

"Wait. One more thing," Tyler says just as I put my foot on the first step.

"What's up?" I ask.

When I turn back to see him, he gets down on one knee and opens a black ring box, revealing a brilliant diamond ring.

My mouth drops open and for a moment I don't believe my eyes.

"Isabelle, I have loved you since we were children. You're my best friend and my first love. I've never stopped feeling that way for you. I thought I did, but now I know that I was a fool. For the last year, I tried to forget you. Forgive, and forget you, but I couldn't."

He stopped talking for a moment and clears his throat. I realize that he's getting choked up.

"I love you. Always have. Always will. Will you marry me?"

My eyes don't leave his. Tears well up and one runs down my cheek. When I want my mouth to say yes, nothing comes out.

I nod my head vigorously and finally manage to whisper, "Yes. A million times yes!"

The rain picks up and every part of me gets wet. I can even feel it in the soles of my feet and the back of my bra. My jacket isn't exactly waterproof and the rain beats at us all the way back to the dock.

Tyler encourages me to go down to the cabin, but I can't leave my new fiancé so soon. Instead, I stand by him near the wheel and hold him tightly.

"Why did you ask me like that?" I ask when we finally talk and head downstairs to change.

"What do you mean? Wasn't it romantic?"

"Yes, of course it was. On the sailboat in the middle of a rainstorm. I'm definitely never going to forget it."

"Well, good. That was the point."

"What exactly?"

"I wanted to give you something positive to associate with the rain. I know that you're not the biggest fan and now you'll have something wonderful to think about every time you see some clouds on the horizon. Think about me and know that I love you more than anything in the world. It's never going to change."

Drenched from head to toe, he rubs his face with a towel and then smiles at me that sexy way that I can't resist.

Before I know what I'm doing, I wrap my arms around him and kiss him. It takes him a moment to realize what is happening, but then he quickly reciprocates.

This time, we don't hesitate. We don't take our time.

Our bodies are fervent and out-of-control. We are rushing, but we are not rushed. There is no savoring the moment.

Our bodies have to be right next to each other or… I'm not sure what's going to happen.

We peel off our clothes and drop them to the floor. I touch his skin. It's slick and soft. I kiss him lightly, but then harder.

Our mouths bind to each other's and we don't let go. He pushes me against the wall and I push against him. He lifts me up and opens my legs.

Slowly, he lowers me over him and then starts to slide me up and down.

I have never been held like this before. I have never been so manhandled and played with, but in that way that you really want. He kisses my mouth, my cheeks, my neck.

He drops one of my legs to the ground and kisses my breasts. He puts one in his mouth while caressing the other. He wanders his fingers down my stomach and towards my clit.

He presses it, he plays with it, and I tilt my head back with pleasure. He pulls out and then gets down on his knees, opening my legs wide.

His mouth and tongue find their way inside and I press myself harder against the wall, trying not to scream.

When I feel like I'm getting close, I start to moan, and he pulls his fingers out of me.

He throws me over the counter. I grab onto it with both hands and part my legs further apart. He slides right in, holding on to my hips.

We move together as one. All movements become like a dance, as if we're listening to the same music.

Whenever I start to feel close, he speeds up to match my movements.

When I try to make it last a little longer, he slows down to accommodate. It's almost as if he knows exactly what I need and what I want.

Finally, I can't hold on anymore. The orgasm washes over me like a wave, only one that emanates from deep inside of me.

He consumes me. It throws me off balance. I moan and collapse onto the counter and then, somewhere in the distance, I hear him moan as well.

"I love you," he whispers into my ear a little too loudly as his breathing slows down.

8

TYLER

It's hard to say goodbye and we tried to prolong it as much as possible. She packed her bags and looked around the boat one last time as I busied myself with something up on the deck to stop myself from feeling the pain of seeing her off.

This weekend was magnificent. It was everything that I never knew I could have again.

That's why I asked her to marry me.

I want to tell her how I feel and I wanted it to mean something.

I wasn't sure if she was going to say yes even though she had said that she would earlier. There was still hesitation and uncertainty that made my stomach twist. I couldn't let her leave without telling her how I felt. The truth is that I want her to be my wife.

We spoke briefly about the future and I know that she's willing to move here. Perhaps it's the best decision. I do have this big marina complex to take care of and she could start her business here. She would have to sell her house, but it's not like she loves living in Pittsburgh.

The one thing that we have not talked about much is her mother. I know that her addiction gnaws at her. I know that she can't forget the love that she feels for her mom, particularly when she is sober.

I know what it's like to have people like that in your life. My father was an addict also. It wasn't really alcohol or drugs, but anger. For a while, things would be great, but then something would set him off and he would become the tyrant. The problem was that you never knew what the thing would be that set him off.

Maybe that's not the best comparison. Isabelle's mom is struggling with a disease that makes her a completely different person when she is drunk or high. I know that if she were to get sober again, Isabelle would have a hard time pushing her away.

That's the whole point of rejecting her now; the hope that they will reconcile sometime in the future when she gets back on the right path.

What's going to happen when her mom gets sober?

Will she regret moving to Seattle?

Will she invite her to visit?

Perhaps. Perhaps not. There is no telling how long the sobriety will last. Maybe a month, six months, a year. Maybe forever.

This might be the one that sticks. There's no way to know for sure. The one thing that I do know is that despite how much I want to protect Isabelle and to tell her that she should just cut all ties with her mom forever, it's not my place.

She should cut all of her ties for now until things change. People do quit drinking. They do quit doing drugs and they do quit gambling.

Even the most unlikely people, the most far gone addicts, are capable of change and it's not my right to discourage her from having a relationship with her mom if she does change.

We haven't talked about any of this. This is just what I think about as I drive her to the airport. I should think about all the nice times we've had together and how lucky we are to be together again, but my thoughts are gloomy and dark. The few times that the sun peeks out, don't make them any better.

The goodbye is tearful and painful. I walk over to get her ticket and then over to the security check line.

I can't go any further and partly I'm glad that I don't have to sit with her by the gate and watch her get on that plane.

I'd rather not be here at all. I would rather just drop her off at the curb because the longer that this process is, the harder it becomes.

Of course, we promise to call, text, and video chat as much as we can. This isn't how it used to be before when all you could do is talk on the phone and even that, do so only occasionally, but I can't take myself back all of those years.

I'm here now and all I feel is pain. Video chat is great, I'm glad that I'll be able to see her and to talk to her in real time, but it's not enough.

I want her near me. I want to smell her.

I want to taste her. I want to feel her.

When I laugh, I want to laugh along with her. I don't want to do it through a screen.

"I'm going to really miss you," I whisper into her ear. "I love you. Always."

"I love you too. Always," she says, swallowing back tears.

Finally, I pull myself away.

There isn't much of a line and she walks right up to the guard who checks IDs prior to going through the metal detector. When she puts her suitcase on the conveyor belt, she waves to me one last time. I wave back and then force myself to walk away.

The rest of the day is a blur. I want to go to bed and bury my face under the covers, but I force myself to go straight to the hotel from the airport.

I don't have any definitive work but being busy and distracted is a good thing. I know that if I were to go back to the boat, all I would feel is the emptiness of the place without her and I'm not ready for that.

Luckily, there is one emergency after another at the hotel. One of the guests is unhappy with their room and moves to another.

Another complaint about the dust on the ceiling fan and the general cleanliness of the room. I end up giving her a significant discount.

After checking on the issues, I realize that this place needs a lot of work. I walk through at least ten rooms, following a checklist, and find all sorts of problems.

Light bulbs missing.

Dust on top of the television.

I even check for stains with a UV light and find things on the headboard and the toilet seat that look a lot like semen.

I meet with everyone in one of the unused dining rooms and go over what I have found. None of the housekeepers are happy but only a few look embarrassed about their quality of work.

"I realize that this isn't so much your fault as it is the fault of the manager who is responsible for teaching you the right things to do and checking to make sure the room is completely clean. Now that Tim is gone, I'm going to be that person."

I hand them each a laminated checklist and an erasable marker. They were supposed to get these already but I'm not sure if they ever did.

I ask them to go back through the rooms that are still unoccupied and check the work that they have all done.

About two hours later after they're done, I go through them as well and find a number of other problems.

We have another meeting and this time I actually walk into the rooms and show them all the issues that I have spotted. None of them seem happy to be there, but they are all getting paid for their time and I intend to get this issue sorted out.

Finally, another couple of hours later, I'm satisfied. I tell them that we will be doing this again tomorrow and the next day, but the more thoroughly the rooms are cleaned, the less time all of this will take up.

I finally get home around nine that evening, spent and exhausted. All of the work at the hotel has successfully taken my mind off Isabelle, but as soon as I'm back on the boat and smell the perfume that she accidentally left behind, everything comes back and I miss her more than ever.

9

TYLER

Isabelle texts when she gets in, but she's too tired to talk. I'm exhausted to, but I can't keep my eyes closed.

My mind keeps ping-ponging from one thing to another and all of the unknowns that I face in my future.

Then, around one in the morning, my phone rings. I answer it expecting it to be Isabelle.

I recognize his deep voice scratched up by years of smoking.

"I'm sorry to call you so late, but I wanted to tell you what happened myself. My attorney is going to call your attorney in the morning and notify him of the news."

"What's wrong?"

"My sons and my wife had a hearing and they were successful in convincing the judge that I'm incompetent."

"Oh my God, I'm really sorry."

"Yeah, you work all your life and this is what happens. It's not good enough for them that they are going to inherit it all, they want it now."

"What are you going to do? What does this mean?"

"Well, I can still walk around and I don't have to go live in some facility. My attorney tells me that I should be grateful for that."

"That's good, I guess."

"Not good enough," Mr. Elliott says.

I hear the familiar ring of the phone and see that he is trying to connect via FaceTime. I accept.

He looks tired and worn out, not so much by a rough night but by disappointment. There are big bags under his eyes and his hair is tossed.

"The judge said that I can't make any more business decisions on my own and that he's giving power of attorney to my oldest son and my wife. Those two have never liked each other. The good thing is that I won't be around to see how that goes."

"What do you mean?" I lean closer to the screen. My heart skips a beat.

Is he really saying what I think he's saying?

Is he contemplating suicide? Is that why he's calling me?

"Don't look at me like that," Mr. Elliott says with a smirk. "I'm not thinking about ending things. I have a long life to live."

"Good," I say, letting out a sigh. "I want you to know that a lot of people care about you."

"Well, that's a lie, but I do know that a few do."

"So where are you now? Are you home?"

"Hell no," he laughs and then coughs mildly, covering his mouth with his elbow.

When the coughing fit subsides, he looks up at me, raising one eyebrow, and says, "I'm in Paris."

“You are in France?”

“I may not have access to my businesses anymore or any of the official money that my wife and I have shared, but luckily, I've been putting a little bit away over the last fifteen years just in case.”

“Just in case of this?”

“No, I couldn't have predicted this, but I did think that maybe one of these days I might just divorce her and having learned from what happened in my previous divorce, I started up a little secret fund to keep me in a lifestyle to which I have become accustomed.”

“Oh, wow,” I say, taken by surprise.

“I have to tell you, son, it's never *not* a good idea to have a secret Swiss bank account.”

I give him a nod, realizing that his reason for this call is not so much to complain or to warn me about what happened, but rather to brag.

“So, what are you doing in Paris?”

“Helene lives here. I told you about her.”

“Yes, the letters.”

"Her children are grown now and mine are backstabbing assholes, so I showed up here and I'm staying indefinitely."

"Well… I'm happy for you," I say which I'm certain is exactly what he wants to hear.

"Anyway, I know that it's late there and I don't want to keep you up, I just wanted to let you know myself, what happened at that hearing today."

"I really appreciate it."

"I know that fighting my sons on this deal is going to be an uphill battle and you really have to think on whether you're up to it. Maybe you should not be. Maybe it's better to just give them what they want and to walk away and live life on your terms. It's up to you."

I nod.

"The only reason why I'm saying any of this is that you really have to figure out what you want to do. Maybe this place is the right place for you, maybe it's not.

Whatever you decide, make sure that it's something that makes you feel alive. There's too much in this life that requires sacrifice and the abandoning of your dreams.

I've lived a lot of years and I sometimes look back and say, 'why the hell did I do all of that? Why the hell did I stay married for so long to a woman I did not love?

Why the hell did I spend so much time building a business that didn't really give me that much passion?' Think about it. I know that you're the right person to run the Elliott Marina and Hotel, but that doesn't mean that it's the right thing for you."

When I hang up, I don't know exactly where to go from here. If the judge has sided with the sons about his competence to make this decision, I know that I don't have much of a case.

I haven't owned the place for very long and I haven't invested much into it either. There's a big likelihood that the judge is going to overturn it and give the marina back to them.

I can fight it, but now that Isabelle is back in my life, is it still something that I really want to do?

When she was here, she mentioned taking the boat out to some warm waters. The Caribbean. Hawaii.

Why not do that?

Why not just have the adventure of a lifetime? Once the hotel decision is reversed, the money will be returned to me and that's a lot more than you ever need to live on a boat.

Who is to say that we can't just take a year to do that?

To get to know each other, to spend as much time together as possible?

Away from the rest of the world?

God knows that we have both been through so much and are due for some quiet time and relaxation.

The sun peeks over the horizon and a new day is just beginning. I rub my hand over the empty spot next to me and I know that the one thing that I want most in this world is to be with her.

Every day, every night, all the time. I want to know what she's thinking.

I want to know what makes her laugh. I want to stop her from crying. I want to make the world a better place for her.

I want to create our own little space in the universe where no one can hurt us and no one can reach us.

I know that she's taking a chance being with me, an escaped convict on the run. I know the authorities will always be looking for me and that we will always have to be on guard.

People like me are found twenty, thirty years later and are brought to court and shackled with gray hair and long white beards.

I don't intend on being one of those guys. I don't intend on watching my wife cry as they haul me off to prison for the rest of my days.

That's why I have to continue to be careful, extremely careful, and that's why I have to make other plans with other possibilities.

I've been thinking about this for a while. The authorities will keep looking for me unless something changes. There is evidence that was not there and I have an alibi that I haven't used.

There must be other evidence as well. Perhaps DNA evidence that they haven't tested? I could spend some of the money I would get back from the hotel on making my case. In proving that I'm innocent.

On finding evidence and then creating enough public awareness for them to reopen the case or at least consider an appeal in my absence. I don't know about any of the exact legal ramifications of this and what is and what isn't possible.

That's another thing that I have to look into, but if I don't want to keep looking over my shoulder for the rest of my life, especially if I were to start a new one with the woman who I love most in this world, I have to do this.

I have to prove my innocence.

10

ISABELLE

Over the next few days, Tyler and I spent a lot of time talking to each other and texting. He stays busy with the hotel even though it feels pretty futile.

With Mr. Elliott in Paris and officially declared incompetent, there's a slim chance that he's going to keep the place.

Still, he continues to work.

I stay busy as well. I find a few more clients and give free introductory sessions and consultations with them and their parents.

Three more sign-up and if I get a few more clients, I can probably afford to rent a space and actually start working in an office instead of driving to everyone's homes.

There are benefits to both. I charge more if I drive. But I can see more clients if I get an office. But then I'd have a lease. But if I had a lease, I could hire other therapists and actually give myself some time off.

I feel like I'm in a state of limbo though. There are so many unknowns that it's difficult to make any decision one way or another.

Partly, I need to know what's going to happen with Tyler and his marina.

The last time we spoke, while we talked on my drive to Monroeville, Tyler had mentioned something that piqued my interest.

"What if we take a break from life? What if we just get on the sailboat and take off?" he asked.

"To go where?"

"Anywhere. Everywhere. Somewhere warm, tropical, where you can have drinks at a swim up bar and then go snorkeling in a turquoise ocean."

"I like that," I said.

After he mentioned this, we didn't have much time to expand on the idea because I had my appointment. We haven't talked about it since then, but my thoughts keep coming back to it.

What if we did that?

It sounds like a dream, a fantasy even, but when I looked up sailing around the Caribbean and living full-time on a sailboat, a bunch of YouTube videos appeared of people doing that exact thing.

I had watched about twenty of them that night and my dreams were filled with burying my feet in the sand, watching my hair flying around us, standing at the helm of the boat, and wearing nothing but tank tops and shorts all while walking around picturesque Caribbean towns.

“Were you just kidding about what you mentioned earlier?” I ask when we FaceTime later that evening.

Tyler has had a long day at work probably driving the housekeepers mad.

“What are you talking about?” he asks, propping his head up with his hand and leaning closer to the computer screen.

I take a bite of my salad.

The arugula and the kale drizzled in olive oil excite my taste buds and after chewing a bit, I say, "About sailing around. About just taking some time off and heading out into the world, with no particular destination in mind."

"I get the feeling that you're not that into going anywhere north," he says with a smile at the corner of his lips.

"But I am into going somewhere south and maybe east, closer to the equator."

"It was something that I was thinking about for sure. What if we just used the time to get to know each other better. Have some fun. Go on an extended honeymoon."

I nod, taking another bite.

"What do you think about that?"

"I'd love to," I say, looking up straight into his eyes.

His whole face lights up.

A warm smile spreads over his mouth and he shakes his head in disbelief.

“Really?” he asks and a few loose strands of hair fall into his face, making him even more sexy than he already was.

He’s so close to me that I can almost reach out and touch him. In fact, I almost do, but then I collide with the screen.

The truth is that he's not here. He's three thousand miles away.

“I want to kiss you so much right now.”

“Me too,” he whispers.

We stare into each other's eyes for a long time, neither of us saying a word. We talk about the trip and all the places that we could go and all of the things that we could see.

I look up island after island on my phone and show him the beautiful towns and the crystal blue waters. He looks up the best snorkeling and diving spots.

He promises me that he'll teach me how to dive and that I'm going to love it.

I'm three hours ahead and I have an early morning meeting with a potential new client, but I don't want to hang up.

We decide to leave the laptops up instead, to look at each other's faces. I lie down on the pillow, prop my head up with my hands, and look at him.

He sets up his iPad to stream with me so that he can use his laptop to do a little work. I turn off the lights. Eventually I turn away from him and fall asleep to the clicking of his keys.

When I wake up a few hours later to use the bathroom, I rub my eyes and see him asleep facing me. It's almost as if he's right here next to me.

Almost.

11

ISABELLE

The following evening, I finally meet up with Libby. This is the first time that I have seen her since I have been home and we are both excited to finally be together. Her husband is working late and she makes dinner for me and the girls.

On occasion, I regret telling Libby everything about Tyler out of fear of putting his life in danger, but another day, like this one, I'm glad that I did. It's nice to have one person in my life who knows the truth with whom I can talk about all of this.

I offer to have a session with Kylie, but Libby says no. She's too excited to talk to me and to hear what I've been up to.

On the drive over, I have made a few decisions of how much I'm willing to tell her, to protect Tyler's privacy, but to share enough that it feels like the truth.

"So, what did you think about Portland? It has always been my dream to go there."

That was one of the bite lines that I came up with. I knew that I wanted to tell her about the Pacific Northwest, but I didn't want to be so precise as to mention Seattle, so I went with Portland instead.

"It was really rainy, but it was beautiful. Very green and lush. The trees are all evergreen which makes the winters a lot more bearable than here."

"That sounds beautiful," Libby says, setting a large bowl of pasta on the table.

"You would like it. There's a lot of water everywhere. A lot of nature as well."

"Yeah, that's what I thought. I'd love to go there someday."

"You'll have to," I smile.

"Well, I love the show called *Portlandia* and it's set there. Plus, I always wanted to make a pilgrimage out to Forks, Washington, where *Twilight* was set. I'm obsessed with that series, even after all these years."

"Oh my God, I love that!" I say.

"You do? I thought you'd make fun of me."

"No, never. Why would you ever make fun of someone for loving a book? If you don't like it, then don't like it, but don't be an asshole about it."

She gets up from the table and comes over to give me a hug.

"What was that for?"

"I truly appreciate you," Libby says with mist in her eyes. "I can't tell you how embarrassed I sometimes feel for liking those books. Even people who haven't read them always make me feel bad for being a fan. I thought that you would do the same thing for sure."

"No, absolutely not," I say, shaking my head.

I reach over, grab her hand, and give her a tight squeeze.

"You can fangirl about it around me anytime. Now let's eat."

Libby wants to know all of the details about my trip. I want to tell her everything, but I can't be too specific. She already knows too much.

I keep his new name to myself along with the specifics about the new business. I do tell her about Rachel, only I called her Courtney.

“So, he’d started seeing someone? How do you feel about that?”

“I'm not really sure how I'm supposed to feel.”

“You feel how you feel. There is no supposed to when it comes to feelings.”

“I know. I know that I'm not supposed to be upset about it, but I am. I mean, not anymore, but I was.”

“So, what did he tell you about her?”

“He told me that they were together, but he caught her cheating and that he broke things off.”

“I guess she wasn't under that impression.”

“No,” I shake my head. “It clearly didn't seem that way.”

“Do you think that he's lying?”

I shrug.

"You have to consider that Isabelle. Even if it's difficult."

"I know," I say. "Of course, I did, but he seemed… He was… So sincere. Plus, when she walked in on us, he told her right away that she had no right to be there because they had broken up."

"That's good," Libby says, nodding.

"I believe him. I know that maybe someone else wouldn't, but I trust him. From being there with the two of them, I got the sense that they did break up and she just wanted another chance."

Sensing that I don't really want to talk about it anymore, she asks me about what I thought about the Pacific Northwest. I admit that, of course, it is a very beautiful part of the world, but I'm not sure if I could really see myself living there.

"Is that something you two talked about?"

"Yes, he brought it up."

"He did?"

Here is where I hesitate. I'm engaged and I should tell her, but part of me is afraid. There's some news, especially really good news, that you sometimes want to keep to yourself. I have no fear of making that wonderful thing dissipate, but I can't.

I took my ring off before I came here, so I dig into my pocket and pull it out. Libby's eyes light up. Her mouth drops open.

"Oh... My... God! Are you serious?" She looks up at me and then down at the ring and then up at me again. She brings the ring up to the light and stares at it in disbelief.

"This is huge. How big is it?"

"I don't know," I say, shaking my head.

"It has to be at least two carats. Maybe more."

"I don't know," I say with a shrug.

"Okay, but what does this mean? Are you officially engaged? Why aren't you wearing it?"

"I was, I mean, I just took that off to come here."

"Why?"

"I wasn't sure if I wanted to tell you," I say cringing. "I'm sorry about that."

"No worries. This is your news to share at your will."

I nod and put the ring back on my finger. We both look at it and I twirl it around, bringing it up to the light.

"So, are you going to marry him?"

When he asked me, I said yes.

I still want to, but for some reason I hesitate in telling her. It has nothing to do with him. I'm not embarrassed. Not at all.

I don't actually know what is causing this panic. Maybe it's because I'm having a hard time imagining life together. Even the life that I saw back in Seattle, that's not the life that we might have.

Everything is still up in the air.

The one thing that I'm sure of is that he can't move here. This is too close to the prison. This is too close to where everything happened.

People here have long memories and his picture has been plastered all over the news here a lot more than it ever was anywhere else.

"Tell me what you're thinking, Isabelle."

"I'm just worried about what's going to happen. There are so many unknowns. He's free now, but who's to say that it will stay that way. If I were to marry him then I would probably have to go on the run. I'd have to live a secret life. I love him more than anyone else in the world but that's a lot to ask, you know what I mean?"

"I know exactly what you mean," Libby says, nodding her head. She reaches over and puts her hand over mine.

Just then, the girls come over and demand to put *Frozen* on the television. Libby rolls her eyes but agrees.

When she comes back to the table, we finish eating. I start to ask her about what's going on in her life, but then she suddenly looks up somewhere far into the distance.

"What's wrong?" I ask.

"Nothing," she shakes her head. "I was just thinking about something."

I wait for her to explain.

"Well ever since you told me about that podcast about Tyler's case and Mallory Deals, that attorney who is convinced that he's innocent, I have listened to all of the episodes twice and have gone through all of the evidence that he has collected and shared on his website as well as the forums that are devoted to it."

I nod. I know exactly what she's talking about. I have been through all of that myself.

"I had no idea that you were so interested."

"It's not every day that a case you listen to actually touches you personally."

"So, what do you think about it?"

"I think that he's innocent. I also think that the prosecutor and the cops possibly have DNA evidence that they haven't tested and don't want to test to prove his innocence."

"What do you mean? Why do you say that?"

"Someone had mentioned it in one of the episodes. The attorney interviewed one of the clerks at the police department. Everything was very hush-hush. No names given, even the voice was distorted, but he made me think that they have something. Something they didn't disclose to the defense team."

"That's illegal," I point out. "They have shared everything with them."

“Exactly. That's the problem. They're covering up the fact that they have a DNA sample they haven’t tested because they suspect that it belongs to someone else. That's a huge problem, but it's also a really big step in getting his sentence overturned.”

12

ISABELLE

My heart starts to beat a little faster. I smile at the corner of my lips, but I'm too nervous to let myself enjoy the moment.

"Nothing about this is definitive and it's going to be impossible to prove."

"Nearly impossible," Libby corrects me. "You're right. Even if they do have a DNA sample, there's also the possibility that it might belong to him and that it doesn't prove anything."

"He didn't do it," I say, suddenly feeling very sorry for myself and for Tyler.

"I know," she nods. "I mean, I get that feeling because even Deals says that he probably has an alibi. It's all very unclear as to what he was doing right before the murder."

"It's not unclear," I say, shaking my head. "I know exactly who he was with and what he was doing. The problem is that she won't testify. She won't make a statement. After what happened in the desert, she'll never come clean about it."

Libby looks at me puzzled. I have told her bits and pieces about this before, but now that I know that she believes me, I tell her everything about Tessa.

I don't know if I should or shouldn't have. It's just that it's so rare to find someone who believes you or believes something so completely unbelievable that you believe and you can't help but connect with that person and try to build as many bridges as possible.

Libby listens carefully and then pulls out her notebook and even makes notes. She startles me when she does this because I hadn't considered putting any of this in the writing, but she promises me that she keeps this notebook safe and away from anyone who might want to read it.

Even Darren, her husband.

I reach over and look through what she has. They are copious notes that she has taken on the podcast as well as on anything that she found on various sites. She adds my information about Tessa to that.

"You're not going to show that to anyone, right?"

She shakes her head.

Clearly, she's not understanding what I'm trying to get at.

"Like Darren?" I ask quietly.

She looks up at me and narrows her eyes.

"I'm sorry," I whisper. "I don't want to offend you, but this is very sensitive information."

"He knows nothing about this. He knows that I like crime stuff and that I like to take notes about different cases that I investigate over the Internet. This notebook is just like any of the other five that I have on various cases."

She walks me over to her bedroom and opens the top drawer of her dresser where she keeps a stack of notebooks in addition to all of her bras and panties. She shows me the ones about various missing cases and different unsolved mysteries.

"How long have you been doing this?" I ask.

"A few years. It's relaxing. It's something interesting to think about."

"Murder?" I ask.

"Well, it sounds terrible when you say it like that," she says, tossing her head back and laughing. "In a way, yes. I just like watching different programs, listening to podcasts, and watching YouTube videos. I put together a picture of the crime. Different programs have different details and then I go on forums, different Facebook groups, and Reddit and try to figure out if anyone else has any other information."

"What have you found about Tyler's case?"

"Unfortunately, they're not that many people siding with him. Most think that it's an open and shut case of an angry husband killing his wife and her lover after finding them in bed together."

I shudder and rub my shoulders as a cold sweat runs down my spine.

"There's also another problem," Libby says.

"What is it?"

"He's not here. He's not there to actually file for the appeals. He's gone. Missing. I've looked into it a little bit and it's going to be an uphill battle to get them to overturn his sentence. It was already going to be that if he were in prison, but now that he's gone, I'm just not sure what's going to happen."

I nod.

I know this already, she's not telling me anything new.

It's hard enough to overturn sentences of prisoners who were still incarcerated. There has never been a case of an overturned sentence of an escaped convict.

"I think that the best that you can do is try, but I would not let my guard down."

I nod slowly.

I look down at my hands and pick at a loose cuticle. The nervousness in the pit of my stomach goes away. It's not that I'm less nervous now, it's more that I just feel resigned. I

know that there are certain things we can do to try to change the opinion of his innocence especially in the eyes of the public, but that doesn't mean that it's going to change much when it comes to his legal status.

Prosecutors do not like to be proven wrong. The legal system is set up in such a way that once a jury makes a decision, it's practically impossible to change.

Libby leaves me alone on the couch for a few minutes while she helps Kylie with something in the kitchen.

For a person who has never thought of herself as not particularly educated, I'm really impressed by the amount of research that she has done and collected on this case.

I leaf through her notebooks, reading about a 25-year-old woman in a small town in Wyoming who is training for a marathon and went on a run and disappeared, never to be heard from again. People suspected her husband, but they had a good relationship and he has a strong alibi that hasn't wavered in all of his years.

Another journal is devoted to a wife and two children who were killed by her husband. Her husband was having an affair and it's likely that has something to do with it.

In this case, Libby's notes all focus on the evidence pointing to his guilt and she agrees with the court's decision that he was their murderer.

"I wanted to reach out to Mallory Deals again," I say, "but I need some backup."

"I actually did too, but I wanted to ask you about it first."

"Will you do it with me?" I ask. "I'm a little nervous contacting him again. I did before but I made up a persona. I think I have to tell him the truth."

"No," Libby says, shaking her head. "You can't trust him."

I nod.

"Isabelle, I'm serious," Libby says. "It's bad enough that you told me about what happened and how you're involved. You can't have people finding out. That's the quickest way for him to get caught and for you to be sent to jail."

"Me?"

"Aiding and abetting a criminal? If they can't get him, they'll pin it all on you. I have seen it happen before. If you don't turn him in, they'll get angry and they'll make you pay for it."

I swallow hard.

"I have to think about it," I finally say. "Maybe it's not a good idea to do any of this. Maybe we should just leave it as it is."

"That's an option, for sure. Wherever he is now, he's safe. I don't know how long that will last, but at least he is for now. There's a good chance that you'll be safe with him, but what if you're not?"

Her words loom over me on the drive back home. I don't know exactly what to make of them. All I know is that I have to talk to Tyler.

I have talked to him about this before, but a lot of time has passed and I hope that he now has had time to reflect and think about everything with a little bit more clarity.

We are making plans for the future, after all, and those plans aren't just about him. They're about me as well.

13

TYLER

After the Elliott brothers have their father declared incompetent and set up an emergency hearing about the marina, I lose interest in going to work.

Of course, there are changes to be made, but what's the point? My attorney continues to be optimistic, but after a while it seems more like he's just being polite rather than actually convincing.

He continues to write hard worded letters and make demands, but none of that matters. The only thing that we are all waiting for is the hearing.

Originally, it was set for two weeks from the competency hearing, but their attorney managed to have it moved up. They are very worried about what's going to happen to their hotel and property while they wait on this decision.

It makes perfect sense if it were anyone but me, but I'm not going to do anything to physically damage a thing, let alone its reputation. Their father would expect nothing less and I'm a man of my word.

I have heard from Mr. Elliott a few times since that night he called me from Paris. He let his family know that he's all right and well. He even filed for divorce from his wife. His attorneys are taking care of everything, but he is positive that he will not receive much in the settlement due to the results of the competency hearing.

Even if you're going senile, you still have the right to get divorced. However, he no longer has the right to control his assets.

How's that fair?

At the same time, the judge only made a finding about his ability to make business decisions that impact family and that means that he still has the right to travel and go anywhere that he pleases.

I'm not sure exactly how much money he had put away, but it's enough that he's not worried. He sent me a picture via text message of himself and his girlfriend on his yacht in the Mediterranean and then another one at the Monaco Casino.

Much to my surprise, she is actually age-appropriate, only a few years younger than he is and older than his previous wife. Looking at them together, I can see that they're happy.

Perhaps they should have been together this whole time, but life is funny that way. You only know what should have happened after everything else goes wrong.

I continue to talk to Isabelle every day and text throughout. Nowadays, she's much busier than I am. Her business is growing and she enjoys her work. Her clients are recommending their friends and she is taking on more students.

Occasionally, we speak about our plans for the future. The more convoluted the situation gets with the marina, the more I dream about disappearing to the Caribbean with the love of my life.

In fact, now that she's in my life, I don't have this need to stay busy. I'd rather just spend every moment with her.

I imagine waking up early and having a cup of coffee while watching the sunrise together.

I imagine going for a swim in the nude, near some uninhabited sandy beach. Then climbing into bed together and making love.

Maybe falling asleep in each other's arms.

Eating lunch out on the deck, with seagulls and pelicans bopping around.

Lying in the hammock and reading, suntanning, and then sailing away to the next uninhabited island and going snorkeling and diving.

I'm sure that we would get tired of this life eventually, but that wouldn't happen anytime soon.

This is what I think about as I lie on my back in the cabin listening to the rain pitter patter against the glass. The rain near the equator is warm and comforting and as long as I have my love with me, what more could I want?

The day of the emergency hearing, the sun peeks out through the clouds. Expecting that I would have a hard time sleeping, I go to bed at nine the night before and actually sleep for eight straight hours.

When I wake up in the morning, I take a shower and get dressed in a suit and tie. I grab an umbrella along with my briefcase, but I don't need it.

The rays of sunshine are unexpected but extremely welcome. The hearing is not being held at the courthouse, but rather at an auxiliary building nearby. Jacob Sommerdahl, my attorney, is there when I arrive, looking calm, collected, and ready for a fight.

He told me to get here early so that he can go over the case with me and his arguments. He's not someone who is used to losing. I listen intently. Whenever my mind drifts off onto something else, I focus my attention again and again. Right before an assistant opens the door to welcome us into the conference room, I check my phone and I see a message from Isabelle: G*ood luck!*

The meeting room itself is on the fifth floor of a large glass building overlooking Puget Sound. There's an enormous conference table and the judge sits at the head. Everything is being video recorded and there's also a stenographer who is transcribing what everyone says.

The three Elliott brothers sit on the opposite side from me with their attorney. Jacob speaks first. He talks in depth about the conversations that took place between myself and Mr. Elliott. This is all hearsay but is part of the argument. I have already been deposed on this and have given a number of statements about exactly what happened that led up to our business deal. The judge, an elderly man with gray hair and a bored expression on his face, has reviewed all of the evidence.

"Mr. Sommerdahl," the judge says, interrupting him in mid-speech. "I am very well aware of the facts in this case."

"Well, in that case, you can understand our position and the fact that my client has done nothing wrong," Jacob says.

"The problem isn't about what your client did right or wrong, it's about whether Mr. Elliott, the petitioner's father, was in his right mind when he made the business deal."

"Mr. Elliott got a fair price for his property and the businesses. I have all of these comps from other businesses that sold in the area that should give you an estimate of what the marina, the hotel, and the two restaurants could be valued at."

"Again, this case has nothing to do with that. It's not about whether he sold it for a fair price. I will grant you," the judge says.

I know words aren't going to justify just as much as Jacob does. He's not a fool. The reason why he's making all these arguments is that there are no other arguments to make. This whole case is about my ignorance of Mr. Elliott's mental state.

"Listen, Mr. Sommerdahl," the judge says when he's about to speak again. "The way that I see it, this case has very little to do with that. He did nothing wrong when engaging in this deal. The problem is that Mr. Elliott was found to be incompetent and therefore incapable of engaging in business dealings, especially to this degree."

"Excuse me, Judge, I'm sorry to interrupt," I say, unable to bite my tongue any longer. "Mr. Elliott was completely lucid and clear when I met him. We have had a number of discussions about this business and the reason why he sold it to me is that he did not want to sell the company for parts. He did not want the hotel, the restaurants, and the marina to be separated. He started them all at the same time and he wanted someone to run them as one entity. His sons did not want to do that."

"It is clear to me that they did not want to do that because it is not in their best financial interest," the judge says. "It is also clear to me that throughout his life Mr. Elliott was a very keen businessman and made decisions that were almost entirely based on what was best for him financially."

"In this case, this was more important to him than money," I insist.

"Do you have any evidence of that?" the judge asks.

"No, of course not. We talked about this over lunches and dinners."

"Again, do you have any evidence to present?" he presses.

"I didn't record him or anything like that if that's what you're asking."

"The problem is that even if you did have evidence that's what he had wanted, that would be in opposition to how he was his entire adult life. Another judge has found him incompetent and gave power of attorney to his sons and his wife. I'm sorry, but at this point, my hands are tied."

I shake my head. I glance over at Jacob who just gives me a slight shrug.

On the other side of the table I see the three sons smiling from ear to ear. Their attorney hasn't even said a word this whole time and we've already lost.

"You have my condolences, Mr. Beckett," the judge says to me. "I'm glad that we can at least take care of this issue straightaway. I'm glad that you did not invest much money or time into this business and the way I'm going to resolve it is to just undo the sale."

I shake my head and look down at the grain in the dining room table. The table is made from one enormous piece of tree and the grain runs all the way down in a motion as if it were a river.

"You have not started any renovations, is that correct?"

"No, I haven't," I say. "I guess I'm thankful that my attorney warned me about this, but I also wonder if perhaps the decision would go my way if I had actually invested more in the business. Perhaps, it would have been more difficult to overturn."

"That's very good news, Mr. Beckett. It would have made my job a lot more complicated if there were renovations that were started and investments that were made."

I open my mouth to say something, but he anticipates my question.

"No, it would *not* change my decision. Actually, the decision is not really mine. I'm just here to undo the deal that should not have happened in the first place. The property is going to revert back to the family and they are going to return every cent that you paid for it."

I nod.

"You have the money, of course?" The judge tilts his head toward the sons.

Webster Elliot, the oldest, nods his head.

"Yes, of course. We haven't touched a cent since we knew that we were going to be making this claim."

The judge seems satisfied with that answer even though I wonder how truthful that is.

I glance over to my attorney, pleading for some help, but by his facial expression, I know that there is no point. We had already lost before we ever came here. Whatever the case that he was going to plead on my behalf, he never even had a chance.

The judge collects the paperwork in front of him and looks over at me and then at the Elliott brothers and back to me.

"The property is going to go back to the Elliott family and they're going to return the full purchase price back to Mr. Oliver Beckett. Since you have attested that the money is already in the account, this exchange is going to take place within the next 72 hours. I expect to see all of the completed paperwork signed and delivered to my desk by then. The whole deal will be undone and everyone will go back to the way that things were before."

As soon as he says those words, my body goes rigid and I sit completely stunned. I saw this happening before we got here and yet it still catches me by surprise.

Just like that, with a few signatures on a few pieces of paper, the marina and the hotel are no longer mine.

After the judge and the clerk leave, I get up. I look up at the Elliott brothers who have a self-satisfied smirk on their faces.

"You know that your father wanted it this way," I say. "He wanted to keep all parts of his business together. He wanted to have someone to run it just like he did."

"Our father has no idea what he wants," Neil, the youngest one says.

"That's not true. He was completely clearheaded when we talked and he knew exactly what he wanted," I insist. "He told me that none of you cared about this place as much as he did. He told me that you only cared about how much you could sell it off for to strangers."

"Guess what, asshole, you are a fucking stranger," Webster says, his voice getting agitated. "You met him at a bar, you had a few drinks, a lunch and a dinner, and you think that you know someone? You don't know the first thing about him. If he were in his right mind and he knew how much people would offer him for each of those things, he would have sold them in an instant. He is forgetful. He remembers things from the past, but not what they are now. You took advantage of him and you're going to pay."

He's about to say something else, but his other brothers pull him away from me.

My temples start to throb and anger starts to pulse through me, but my attorney pulls me away just before it boils over.

We walk down the hallway and around the corner where we can be apart from the Elliott group. I don't want to follow him, but I do. With my hands balled up into fists, it won't take much for me to run over and punch one of them in the face, but that's just going to make things worse.

So far, I've been lucky. I've managed to buy this property without anyone knowing my true identity and now I've managed to sell it. Forced to sell it, but still.

Walking around the corner isn't enough and I feel my anger hit it's boiling point.

I need to get some fresh air.

Luckily, there's a door that goes out onto a large courtyard and I head straight there.

"I know that this is very disappointing," Jacob says. "I'm upset too, but I told you that this is something that we had to expect."

"Yes, I know," I say, nodding.

"Let's look at the bright side. You didn't invest anything into the property, not really. So, what exactly are you really out? You get all of your money back and you can buy something else, free and clear. Something that will probably be a lot more profitable than that place."

"You are right, of course. I know that. I also know that Mr. Elliott was not incompetent when he made that deal. He sold it to save that place and now his sons are going to ruin it."

"I know. Of course, I know that, but we tried to prove that and we failed," Jacob sighs. "So, we just have to move on. Some things in life are just unfair and there's nothing you can do about it. You're going to drive yourself crazy trying to fix every wrong thing."

I nod and pace in circles. He stands with me for little bit, but after a little while he checks the time and says that he has a meeting to get to. He nudges me to follow him and despite the bitterness coursing through my veins, I do.

We shake hands goodbye in the parking lot. I get into my car and drive back to the boat. I have seventy-two hours before the property becomes theirs, but it will take me less than five minutes to clear out my desk.

I have an office there which I haven't really used, keeping my computer with me and carrying it back and forth from home. Nothing else in there belongs to me, not anymore. I guess I have to tell my employees that I no longer own the place, but that can wait until tomorrow or the day after.

When I get back, I make myself a stiff drink. Then I start the engine and take the boat for a spin around the bay.

I'm tempted to go out further into the ocean, maybe head north to Canada. Once I'm away from everyone, I cut the engine and let out the sails. The wind picks up and it would be so easy to just point myself in one direction and go, never to be heard from again.

But I can't leave yet.

It starts to drizzle that then turns into hail. Hundreds of little balls of ice begin to fall from the sky.

I drop the sail, turn on the engine and head back to the dock.

I'm tired of the cold.

I'm tired of being apart from Isabelle.

I'll go wherever she wants to go.

If she wants to live in Pittsburgh, we can do that. I can find something to do or I can just stay home and wait for her and be with her.

If she wants to go to the Caribbean, we can do that. I thought that this place would be good for me and that I would be good for this place, but things don't always turn out the way that you plan.

In fact, the best things in life may be something you haven't planned for at all.

14

ISABELLE

Ever since I got back from Seattle, I have been eating way too much food. It's almost like I don't have control over anything that I crave anymore. I was being very good with focusing on just eating healthy food until that trip, but after seeing Tyler and getting back together with him, a wave of relief has washed over me and suddenly, I can't stop myself.

Every Sunday I promise myself that on Monday I'm going to watch what I eat and not snack, but that usually lasts until 10 am.

Mondays tend to be complicated. It's when I see the most clients. I rush around, eating meals in my car, and grabbing what I can on the go.

I know that I need to meal plan. I know that I need to keep track of what I eat, but as soon as I have that first so-called cheat meal, I give up and call it a day.

I haven't talked to Tyler about any of this and my insecurity about my own body is mine alone.

I carry it around with me like luggage. It's always there. I can't do anything to get rid of it.

Of course, this morning is no different. I wake up ravenous. My stomach is turning and even though I try to find something healthy, I end up eating a lot of unhealthy things while the food cooks.

I've never been addicted to a substance before like a drug or alcohol, but I wonder if this is what it's like. You just have to have it and there's nothing you can do to stop yourself from getting it.

I look at the time. I don't have much of it left, not if I want to get there. It's too late to take a shower so I just put some dry shampoo in my hair and put on a little bit of makeup. Luckily, I can wear something comfortable to my appointments. No special dressy clothes required.

On the drive over to Monroeville, the rain picks up and the traffic slows down. After a long time in the car, I finally get there, only a few minutes late. My head is pounding from the thunder and the concentration on driving through all of that water.

I again feel nauseous.

I rarely feel this way. I rarely get headaches. I don't really know what's going on with me. The appointment goes well and Taylor, the little girl, is making a lot of progress with her speech.

Her mom complains that she never wants to do any talking outside of these appointments, but that's pretty common. I don't really have much advice except to just hang in there and keep trying.

The mom and I chat for a while after Taylor goes to play. She tells me that she and her husband are trying to have another baby and have had a couple of miscarriages. I offer my support and my condolences. I like that she's so open about it because so few people are. It happens to so many women and yet we rarely talk about it.

A few minutes later, she excuses herself to get a phone call and I go to her downstairs bathroom.

My stomach is cramping up and my headache is back with a vengeance.

I take a few deep breaths and try to figure out what's going on. I'm both hungry and nauseous at the same time. I use the last of the toilet paper and I look for another roll underneath the sink to restock it.

That's when I see two boxes of pregnancy tests. There are about four in each. I guess they have been buying them in bulk.

I grab one of the boxes and read the directions on the back. You basically pee on a stick and then wait a minute for the results to come through.

I have only ever taken one, a long time ago when I was in high school, after my first time. I haven't kept very good track of my periods and even though we used protection, I got scared and worried that I might be pregnant.

I wasn't.

This time, I'm sure that I'm not. I keep track of my periods on an app on my phone and I click on it to double check the last time I had one.

Oh my God, I say silently to myself when I realize that it has been seven weeks since I've had one.

No, this can't be right. I must have just forgotten to enter it.

I try to remember the last time that I had it.

A cold sweat runs down my side when I realize that the app is right. I haven't had a period in almost two months. I make my hands into fists and pump them a little bit to get rid of some nerves. I tap my fingers on the countertop and look at myself in the mirror.

What turned out to be just a possibility, maybe even a joke, was suddenly a very real thing.

I look down at the pregnancy test. There is a big Costco-sized pack of them and I doubt that she would miss this one.

I can't wait.

I sit back down on the toilet and pee on the stick.

Then I put it on the counter.

A minute ticks by.

Then another.

It has been more than enough time, but I can't force myself to look at the result. I have to summon the courage, but I don't have any.

Why didn't I do this with Tyler? Why am I doing this alone?

I take a deep breath and it gets lost in the back of my throat.

"Are you okay?" Taylor's mom asks from the living room. It occurs to me that I have been in here way too long.

"Yes, I'm fine. I'm just not feeling very good."

"Oh no, I'm so sorry. Is there anything I can do?"

"No, I think it might be something I ate. I'll be out in a minute."

"Take as much time as you want." I hear her walk away from the door.

Taylor laughs and *Dora the Explorer* sings somewhere in the distance.

Finally, I force myself to grab the pregnancy test. Instead of a line that I have to decipher, there's just the word that stares straight back at me, *Pregnant*.

I look at it and then I look at it again. I close my eyes and open them, to make sure that I'm reading it correctly. I close the lid and open it back up, but it still says that I'm pregnant.

Of course, nothing about this is certain. I have to go to the doctor and get a blood test to know for sure, but the odds are that I am.

I put the pregnancy test in my purse and come out of the bathroom, my face completely devoid of color.

I can't stay in this house much longer.

I mumble something about having to get back and scramble to my car.

When I start the engine, I reach for my phone and immediately want to tell Tyler, but as soon as I see his name, I hesitate.

He already has a lot to think about. Today is the day of his hearing with the judge and the Elliott brothers. I don't want to worry him.

Besides, I'm not entirely sure how I want to proceed with this. I have never really wanted to have a child, at least not yet, and I'm not sure if I'm ready.

No, I'm certain that we are *not* ready. Everything with Tyler is up in the air. Besides, he's an escaped convict that will always have to be looking over his shoulder. He asked me to marry him and I said yes, but I'm not sure if that is the kind of world that I want to bring a *child* into.

On the way back to my house, I am tempted to cancel the rest of my appointments, but I stop myself.

I need something to do that isn't dwelling on this. I need something positive that I can think about.

Later in the afternoon, Tyler calls me and tells me the bad news. He lost the property. The sale is going to be reversed. The Elliott brothers have to pay him back the full purchase price and he has to return the marina, the hotel, and two restaurants back to the family.

When he tells me this, his voice is monotone and distant.

"What do you think about this?" I finally ask.

I thought that he would be a lot more frantic or out-of-control, but I can tell that he has had some time to process it.

"I'm not sure what to think," Tyler says. "I guess it is what it is. I'm glad I didn't invest more into the building or start any big construction projects like I wanted to."

"I'm still really sorry about it," I say. "I know that you wanted it to be your fresh start."

"Yes, but that was before… You and me, and us."

I smile looking at his weary face in the video chat. He smiles back at me, but his eyes look somewhere past me, distracted, like he's not really here.

"So, what's going to happen?"

"In three days, the deal is undone and we all go our own way."

"What does that mean for you?"

"I don't know," he says, shaking his head. "What do you want it to mean for me?"

I shrug and say, "I don't know what we can and can't do."

"We can do anything," he says. "The thing we talked about? Sailing around the world? Sailing to the tropics? We can do that if you want. Do you?"

"I do," I say. "Of course I do."

He smiles and I smile too.

"Listen, this has all been very long and complicated and I'm feeling a little bit worn out. Do you mind if I take a nap and we can talk about this later?"

"Of course not," I say and give him an air kiss for goodbye.

I hang up the phone and stare at the blank screen. Just as one thing seems to be figured out, there's a curveball.

Is this what life is like? It wasn't at all like this before I met Tyler.

Everything was planned out simple and methodical, but now?

There are of course elements of my old life that I miss. I liked the predictability.

I liked knowing what happens, when, and why. That hasn't been the case with Tyler.

Will it ever be like that with him? In reality, he's a pretty easy-going guy. He doesn't demand too much and he doesn't push me into doing things that I'm not comfortable with, but he is still who he is and the fact that he has to live a secret life is something that I have to consider.

It's one thing for me to go into this world and sign up to be with someone like him, but is it really fair to do that to my child?

Our child?

What happens if our baby is four years old and Tyler gets arrested and sent away to prison for life?

What kind of life would that child have?

What kind of time and memories would he have with his father, visiting him in a maximum security prison where he couldn't even give him a hug?

No, I can't have that. I can't bring someone into this world and into so much uncertainty.

Instead of getting into bed, I grab a big blanket from the couch, bundle up, and go sit in the rocking chair out on the back porch.

It's early evening, twilight, and everything is overcast and gray. It looks like I'm back in Seattle except for the trees are naked and barren.

This isn't exactly the best time to sit out in the backyard and yet there's something peaceful about being out here.

Somewhere in the distance a few birds sing and there's a groundhog that runs through my yard checking to see if I'm growing anything delicious.

I'm not. I don't have much of a green thumb.

I rub my stomach and eat a cracker that makes it rumble a little bit less.

Of course, this could all be a mistake. I could actually not be pregnant at all, but these are important things to consider. Tyler asked me to marry him and I said yes.

When I did that, I was just thinking about our life together. I was thinking about all the fun that we could have, all the places that we could go and see.

I wasn't thinking about building a life with a felon, a man convicted of murdering his wife and her boyfriend. I know that he didn't do it and I know that a few people believe that as well, but if I have his child in my womb, I have to make *everyone* know the truth.

He did not commit that heinous crime. Somebody else did and that means that we have to find out the truth. Then we have to tell anyone who will listen about what really happened.

I know that this is something that I have to do. The problem is that I'm not sure that Tyler is on board with that. He has a new name, new identity, and new life.

He feels safe when he really shouldn't.

I found out where he was and that means that someone else can too. His world is built on shifting sands.

If he wants to start a life with me, and I think that he does, we have to build a stronger foundation. We have to be smart and safe.

We have to prove what really happened to his wife and who really committed that murder.

15

ISABELLE

When Tyler and I talk later that evening and the following morning, we talk mainly about him and our plans for the future.

I want to tell him about the pregnancy test so badly, but I bite my tongue. I made an appointment with the doctor for later this afternoon and I want to make sure that I'm actually pregnant before we start having all of these conversations.

Besides, I'm still buying myself some time.

I know that Tyler needs to know and I will tell him, but I wanted to sleep on the decision to see how I actually felt about it. This is my body and it has to be right for me.

I have never considered being a mom before. Lots of women grow up imagining their lives as mothers, but I never thought about that before. It's silly to say that, especially given the fact that I work with children, but for some reason they always seem to belong to other people, not to me.

I know what happens to women when they become mothers. Of course, there are some that can have it all, as the saying goes, but for the most part, we are the ones who are stuck taking care of the child and letting our dreams fall to the wayside.

That wouldn't necessarily have to happen to me, right? I already got my degree in speech therapy and I started a new business. I can keep getting new clients and teaching the kids for as long as I can. It wouldn't interfere with my life as I know it.

But what about afterward? After the baby is born?

When I get to the appointment, the nurse at the front desk tells me that I was lucky to get it because usually they are booked two to three weeks in advance, if not more, but someone had canceled and I just happened to call.

I say thank you, but she still doesn't seem satisfied. I don't know what she wants from me, but I'm too nauseous and uncomfortable to delve into it.

Before seeing the doctor, a nurse hands me a small plastic container and shows me where the bathroom is. I pee into it and then she shows me into a smaller waiting room. Here, there are no magazines, but I keep myself occupied with my phone. Fifteen minutes later a doctor in her early thirties comes in and confirms the pregnancy.

Everything else after that is a blur. I remember telling her that I feel very nauseous and can barely get out of bed in the morning so she writes me a prescription for Diclegis. She tells me that this is basically a slow release of an over-the-counter sleeping pill called Unisom and B12 vitamins.

She has a sample and I take one. I slowly feel better. She tells me to eat crackers and to try to keep something in my stomach at all times.

Finally, the appointment is over. As soon as I get back to my car, I regret the fact that I didn't tell Tyler and burst into tears because he wasn't there with me.

I know that my emotional state has a lot to do with my hormones but knowing something like that doesn't change how you feel. I barely force myself to drive to the pharmacy and pay an exorbitant amount for the medication, which is not approved by my insurance.

It's $500, but I pay for it because I can't bear being this nausea anymore. Besides, I'm not in the best state to make financial decisions. When I finally get back home, I crawl into bed only to get right up and run to the bathroom when the nausea gets too bad.

On television and in movies, women throw up a few times and then go on with their days as if nothing has happened. They don't show my puffy face or the splotchiness on my skin. They don't show me crawling back to my bed and contemplating how much energy I would need to walk all the way to the kitchen to get something to eat.

I try to remember whether I have bread or crackers in the pantry and on what shelf they are. Standing upright makes me feel dizzy as if I'm riding a roller coaster and I can't maintain that position for long. All of a sudden, I also feel incredibly weak, the weakness starting out somewhere at the nape of my neck and spreading throughout my body.

What I really want right now is some toast. For some reason, the bread just isn't doing it for me, but if it were toasted with oil on the skillet, I feel like I could actually get it down and it would make me feel better.

No one is here. No one can help me. I pull the chair up next to the stove so that I don't have to stand, but I quickly start to feel sick again. It's not just the vomiting, but also the diarrhea that comes at the same time and I suddenly have to decide between which one to expel first.

I give up on the toast making, grab a loaf of bread, and climb into bed. I drink a little bit of water, but my lips are still dry and my mouth is parched like the desert. A few hours later, Tyler texts me and calls. I'm too weak to answer, but I manage to message back.

Another couple of hours later, he calls again. We haven't missed one evening of video chatting, but if I answer him now and he sees how I am, he'll know that something is wrong. I decide to tell him later.

Maybe I'll feel better tomorrow?

He doesn't take no for an answer. He keeps texting me and asking to at least talk on the phone.

When he calls again around ten that evening, I answer, not having the energy to text him instead. Just then, he clicks the video chat button and I see it coming through on my end. I reach over to Decline, but my finger slips and hits Accept instead.

"What's wrong? Are you okay?"

I look at my face in the small rectangle at the top. My mascara is smeared all the way down my cheeks. My skin is sallow and white. My hair is dented and out of control.

"I'm fine," I mumble, my voice weak and distant.

"What happened?"

I'm tempted to lie. I'm tempted to just tell him that I have the flu.

It would work.

He'd believe me.

But the words, "I'm pregnant," just slip out of me.

16

TYLER

She has been avoiding my calls this whole day. At first, I thought that she was busy, actually busy, but then I realized that there's something else. When I press the button to FaceTime, I'm actually surprised that she answers.

She looks tired. Exhausted. Her eyes are swollen. She looks like she has the flu, but then I ask her what's wrong and she says the last thing that I expect to hear.

The words, "I'm pregnant," ring in my head as if they were the sound of a bell. I stare at her, not exactly processing what she is saying.

"How could this be? How could you be pregnant? We were so careful."

I go over every time that we were intimate and whether or not we had used protection. We have, as far as I can remember.

I know that condoms are not one hundred percent safe, but they are 99.9% effective.

So, how could this be happening?

"Why are you so sick?" I blurt out.

She looks at me and I realize immediately that is not the right reaction.

"I have morning sickness," she moans. "The only problem is that it's been going on the whole day."

So that's why she hasn't been very talkative recently. It all makes sense.

"How did you find out?"

She lays back down on her back and puts one hand over her forehead. I can see the beads of sweat and the discomfort that she's feeling. Her voice is soft and every word is difficult to say, laborious, even. She seems to be out of breath even though she's barely moving.

"Sorry, I have to lay this way otherwise my head starts spinning." She lays absolutely flat on her back, pointing the phone at her chin.

"It's okay. I just wish that there were something that I could do."

"Me too," she mumbles.

"So, what happened?" I ask.

"I had my meeting with Taylor and I started to feel really sick. I thought that it was something that I ate, like maybe that I had food poisoning, but when I was in the bathroom, I saw that they had a few packets of pregnancy tests and for some reason I just decided to take one."

"You had no idea that you might be pregnant?"

"I usually keep track of my period on my phone, but I must've forgotten last month. That's when it happened."

"So, are you sure?" I ask. "I mean, maybe you should go to the doctor…"

"I have already been to the doctor," she says quietly. "That's where I went this morning. They gave me a blood test and they confirmed that I'm pregnant."

"Wow," I whisper.

We don't say anything for a while. She puts the phone down and points it at the ceiling. The fan is on and I can see the shadow vibrate from its spinning.

I'm not really sure what to say. I've never been in this position before. I thought about wanting to have kids in a very hypothetical way. I knew that people my age were having them, but it never really occurred to me that I could be one of them.

Now, just as the idea settles a little bit more in my mind, I start to feel an inkling of excitement. I know that this isn't the right time and it's not the best thing for the child to have a father with a secret life, but we are in love.

We care about each other.

We respect one another.

What more could a child want than for their parents to love one another and to love them?

Isabelle picks up the phone and points it at her face. Her makeup is smeared under her eyes and she looks weary and exhausted. Her skin is extremely pale and her lips are chapped.

Still, she has never looked more beautiful.

"I'm really sorry about everything," she says, her voice cracking.

"What are you sorry about? What do you mean?"

"I know that this is my responsibility. I should have kept track of everything better. This shouldn't be happening to us."

"I know maybe this isn't a good time, but what if it is? We love each other. We're going to get married. After they reverse the sale, we're going to have more than enough money to raise this child."

"So… You're actually into it?"

"I think so," I say. I think about it for a moment and then nod more definitively. "I am."

"I never knew that you wanted to have kids."

"I wasn't sure if I did. It always seemed like something other people did, but why not? I love you and you love me. We have plenty of money."

"What about your… past?"

I shake my head, not sure what she's getting at.

She swallows hard and sits up, propping herself up with pillows. I can tell that this takes a lot of energy and I give her time. She takes a sip of water and bites down on a cracker.

"I want to have a child with you too," she says slowly. "There's something that gives me pause. Besides being so sick, of course."

I nod and wait for her to continue. She inhales deeply and exhales very slowly.

I look straight into her eyes, but she avoids mine. I wonder what her hesitation could be. I wonder if it's something that we can survive.

She licks her lips and I wait for her to say something, but she doesn't.

"What is it?" I ask. "What are you thinking?"

"Your past. It's always going to haunt us. I know that you have this whole new life now and it's relatively safe for now, but what if someone finds out? What if when our child is five or six or twelve or fifteen, something happens and you're sent away to prison?"

"That's not going to happen," I say, shaking my head.

"You know that it's a possibility."

I shake my head and pick at the grain in the dining room table.

"I'm not sure what you want me to say. Yes, it is a possibility."

"That's what worries me. That's what I'm afraid of."

"What can I do about it? This is who I am, Isabelle."

"No, it's not. You're an innocent man convicted of a crime he didn't commit. He managed to escape and run away and to start a new life. That's great, but you have to clear your name. You have to do something to make people believe that you didn't do that terrible thing. That way if you are ever caught again, the public will be on your side."

I swallow hard.

She's right. I know that.

I'd thought about it a number of times before. The thing about my past is that it's in the past. I was so traumatized by what happened that it's almost easier for me to just leave it there rather than dredge it up and think about it.

Even when Isabelle was trying to get me to listen to the podcast by that Mallory Deals guy who believes that I'm innocent, I couldn’t do it and I haven't since then.

Here's a man who believes that I'm telling the truth and I should be running toward him with open arms, yet I have shut him out.

Why?

It's too painful to relive what happened in prison. It's too painful to relive what happened leading up to the trial.

A lot of people think that if they were arrested for a crime they didn't commit, they would want to spend their whole lives proving everyone wrong. I did as well.

Then I got a chance to run away. To literally escape all of my problems and become someone else.

Once I did that, I couldn't go back. I can’t face my old self because that would be bringing back all of that trauma and all of that disappointment.

I tell Isabelle all of this in as few words as possible. She listens carefully and when she nods, I know that she understands and sympathizes. I also know that she's right.

I don't know how far I can get with the prosecution and I doubt that they'll ever believe me, but I have to start making a case for my innocence.

Tessa was my alibi, but there may be more.

Somebody did kill my wife and my business partner.

Who? I have no idea.

Why? I also have no idea.

The only thing that I know is that I did not do those things and that I got blamed for their deaths.

No matter what they did or how much they hurt me, they didn't deserve what they got and I don't deserve to be called a murderer.

"I'm not sure where to start," I say.

"We have to reach out to Mallory Deals," Isabelle says.

"Reach out how? I can't reach out to him."

"No, you can't, but I can. I already did."

"What?" I gasp.

"I used another name. I didn't tell him anything personal but maybe I should. I can tell him as much of the truth as possible. You and I were friends growing up and that I'm very interested in this case because I don't think that you did it."

"Then what? What can he do?" I ask, carefully considering the option.

"I've been going through his website and listening to the episodes. He really suspects that the prosecution has some DNA evidence that they did not test. If that's the case, then that's our best starting point."

Even talking about these details makes me sick. It's almost as if it brings back my old identity and pushes it in my face, front and center.

I don't want to be that old guy. I want to be able to construct this new self and begin again with a wife and newborn baby.

"I know that it's hard for you," Isabelle says after a long pause. "I know that you don't want to face what happened. I know that you're innocent and I believe you. Why should it matter if others do as well? It just does. We have to set this case up in such a way that if they ever find you then we at least have a chance of gaining your freedom."

"We have this whole new life," I say. "I have a new identity and no one knows who I am except for you. Why not just take the money I'll get for the hotel and go live anywhere we want?"

"We can do that," Isabelle says. "This is just a safety precaution. I don't want to take our child to kindergarten and then come home and find out that I'm never going to see you again. You didn't commit those crimes. I know that it's difficult for you to go back to that time when they arrested you and all that time that you served in prison, but you have to. You have to prove your innocence and you have to show them that they were wrong. You have to make people believe your story. It's believable. It's true."

"Why would that change anything though? If they come for me and if they find out where I am and what I'm doing, it won't matter what anyone believes."

"That isn't true," she says, shaking her head. "Public opinion is important. It has the power to change people's minds. It has some power to put pressure on prosecutors. Besides, the people working in that police department and the prosecutor's office might be different now than they were back then. Who knows what kind of corruption and basic incompetence led to your conviction. We need to find out."

I know that she's right. I've been thinking about it myself lately.

The problem is that I've been living so simply day to day, that I haven't given much thought to the future.

With asking her to marry me, things have changed. I want more from life. I want to make plans.

I want to make a life with the woman I love and for that I need certainty about what may or may not happen in the future.

"I think you're right," I finally relent. "We have to at least figure out if it's possible to prove my innocence."

A wave of relief washes over her.

"That's all I want," she says. "I want to find out what's possible. If it's just a lost cause then we can just double down and never talk about this again, but I want to give it a real shot, Tyler. I love you and I want to make sure that this child is protected and has both its' mother and father."

My thoughts go back to the baby that's growing in her belly.

We have talked so much about my past and what it means for this future child of ours, we haven't actually talked about the consequences of having a baby.

"So, how are you feeling? What are your thoughts about everything that has happened? How did this even happen?"

"I guess we weren't as careful as we thought we were," she jokes. "To be honest, though, I was scared. I am scared. I wasn't sure that I was cut out to be a mom, given the terrible example of motherhood that I have had."

"You're going to be an amazing mother."

"I hope so. I know that you're going to be an amazing father."

People say that all the time to their spouses and their significant others, but in this case, I really mean it.

Isabelle is kind, loving, and not self-centered. Those are the best qualities you can have in a mother.

She's present and thoughtful. I just hope that I can live up to being as good a father as she will be a mother.

We don't say anything for a while and just look into each other's eyes.

"There's a lot of responsibility in bringing a child into the world," I finally say. "I think that the biggest gift you can give them is to give them parents that love each other and care about each other. We have had a lot of obstacles stand in the way of our being together, but we overcame them and stood as one anyway. There's no one that I would rather spend my life with but you, Isabelle. You understand me and get me on that primal level that no one else does. You get my jokes and you understand how I feel without me even saying it out loud."

"I love you, Tyler," Isabelle says. "I can't wait to marry you and to spend the rest of my life with you, wherever it takes us. Finding out that I'm pregnant makes me realize that it doesn't matter where we live or what we do, all that matters is that we're together and that we go through these things with one another."

I smile at her and she smiles back. Her smile fills up the whole screen.

"You know, I was thinking about something else," she adds.

"What?"

"I was thinking of taking you up on your offer."

I tilt my head, not sure what she's talking about.

"You wanted to take me around the world, right? On your sailboat? I think I want to do that, too."

A FEW DAYS LATER, we both settle into the idea of having a baby. We play around with different names and I promise to come out to Pittsburgh as soon as I can after the deal is reversed.

I start to feel incredibly lucky about what happened with this marina purchase and I become not so secretly glad that the Elliott brothers actually got control of it. I'm going to get all of my money back and I can start a new life with the love of my life.

I go back to the hotel, collect my things, and say goodbye to all of the staff members. Some look sad, but most barely notice. I haven't really played much of a role in this place, at least not as much as I wanted to, but perhaps it's fine that it's going back to the family.

Mr. Elliott, of course isn't pleased, but again he's not my problem. He's in France with his mistress, living on the secret funds that he had stashed away from his family.

When I tell him that my fiancée is pregnant, he tries to give me advice and to tell me to keep some of my money in a secret account as well.

"I appreciate your help," I say, "but I love her and things are different between us."

"I know that you love her. That's why I'm telling you to do this. It's the women that you love that are going to fuck you over the most."

At this point, Mr. Elliott has become something of an older uncle to me, giving out unsolicited advice that I have to listen to, but I don't mind.

I don't have a family and it's kind of nice to have an older, fatherly figure in my life. After we hang up, I pack up what's left of my office into a box and head out to the car.

They are waiting for me right out front.

My heart skips a beat as soon as I see them.

All three Elliott brothers are there along with someone else. When I walk out the double doors, and the guy on the end turns to face me, I recognize him immediately.

"It's nice to see you all," I say this as casually as possible. "Tim, how are you?"

My head is pounding, but I don't betray an inkling of frustration or nervousness. I broaden my shoulders and plaster a casual smirk on my face.

"Anything I can help you with boys?"

"We just wanted to let you know that we know something about you," Webster says.

"That is?" I ask, walking past him and heading to my car. I press the button on the door opener, to pop the trunk. "Listen, the property is yours tomorrow. As long as I have a certified check or wire transfer in my account, you're getting it back exactly as I got it. Actually, a little bit improved."

“No, I don't think so,” Webster says.

“Excuse me?” I ask, putting the box in the trunk and closing it.

“Well, that was our agreement, but things have changed. In fact, I think that you're going to just hand it over to us and we're not going to have to pay you a dime.”

“What makes you think that?” I ask, crossing my arms.

Who the hell do they think they are? I stay calm.

I don't need trouble and I don't want any.

“Well, Mr. Beckett, is it?” Tim walks over to me, cocking his head, full of self-righteousness.

“What do you want?” I glare at him.

“I have it on good authority that your name is not Mr. Beckett all.”

“I have no idea what you're talking about.”

“Really?” He pulls out a wanted poster with my picture on it. “We know exactly who you are, Tyler McDermott.”

Tim shoves the poster up to my face so that I am eye to eye with my old identity.

"What my friend here is trying to say," Alfred, the middle son, says, "is that you have a secret Mr. Beckett, and we intend to help you hold onto that secret, but for a price."

"That price is you walking away from this deal once and for all. We won't pay you a cent and you will tell the court that we paid you every last penny," Neil says.

The four of them stare at me with glee in their faces. They say other things, threatening things, but my head starts to buzz and I can't process a thing.

Finally, one of them presses the poster into my chest and gives me until midnight tonight to make my decision.

17

TYLER

I watch them stroll away from me, full of self-satisfaction. I pick up the wanted poster off the ground and I look at my old face looking back at me.

When it comes down to it, I don't look that different. The only difference is that you don't expect someone like me to be this person from another part of the country living another life.

I have no idea how they found out about me, but apparently, it's much easier than I thought it would be.

I mean, Isabelle found me.

She saw a picture of me in a magazine and came out here on a whim searching for me. What would stop someone else from doing the same thing?

As I climb down into the cabin of my boat, I'm keenly aware of the fact that I can barely feel the tips of my fingers as I grab onto the railing. It's almost as if my whole body is detached from me somehow. It's almost as if I'm not really here.

I walk over to the sink, fill up a glass full of water, and force myself to drink it. After I'm done, I feel a little bit more invigorated and present.

What the hell do I do now?

The Elliott brothers are extorting me. They are trying to get out of paying me nineteen million dollars and they are threatening to expose who I am if I tell the court that they have not paid me.

One option is that I deny what they're saying. I have a legitimate identification and a credit history along with everything else, but the problem is that my fingerprints would not match up.

If this were ever taken to the authorities or presented as a possibility, the way that anyone would prove whether I'm indeed Tyler McDermott is to compare our fingerprints. That's how they would confirm it.

I take a deep breath and go straight to the bedroom to pack. I grab only the necessities and throw them into a duffel bag that I have kept in the closet for this exact emergency.

That's where I have my backup identification. That's where I have a stash of $20,000 in cash along with a couple of burner phones as well as a few other things that I need to start a new life.

I have mentally prepared for this moment and have gone through a number of drills.

What would I do if the cops closed in on me?

What would I do if someone recognized me?

Luckily, the circumstances are not that dire. They gave me until midnight to make a decision and that means that I have hours to get away.

"This could be worse," I say to myself. "This could be like the time that I ran through the drill of what to do with the FBI and the police surrounding this marina. Still, I need to give myself as much of a head start as possible."

Before I walk off the boat, I take one last look around. I wish more than anything that I could go somewhere on it, but since the deal got reversed, I'd have to return the boat to the Elliott family.

I thought that I'd be able to buy another one with the money that I thought that I would get, but now all I have is this twenty grand in my pocket and that's all that I'm going to have for a while.

The boat is a slow style of transportation. Besides, it's registered in my name and after today, Oliver Beckett will cease to exist.

They will look for him, but they won't be able to find him.

When I get to the car, I know that I will have to ditch it as well, but not yet. The cops aren't looking for me and they won't for a while, if ever.

As soon as I start driving, I get on the phone with my attorney and tell him that I have received the money from the Elliott brothers and to release the paperwork to transfer the property back to their name.

Jacob is surprised. He hasn't heard anything back from their lawyers, but I insist that this is what happened.

"They wired it," I say.

"Are you sure that it's in your account?"

"Of course," I lie.

I laugh and act as casual as possible.

"Honestly, I'm relieved. This has been hanging over my head for a while and now I'm just going to take some time for myself to go on a trip."

"Yes, that's probably for the best," he says and I hear the hesitation in his voice. "I'm really sorry that it didn't work out."

"Do I owe you anything else?" I ask, referring to the payment that I have already made to him.

"Thank you for your hard work and all of your help."

When he hangs up, I let out a small sigh of relief. When the traffic slows down, I write down his phone number in a small notebook and toss the phone into a plastic bag that I'm going to throw out the next time I stop.

I have already texted Isabelle about not being in touch for a little while, but she hasn't responded yet. I won't be able to hold onto this phone for much longer than a few hours because I don't want anyone who would trace it in the future to know where I'm headed.

I have a few disposable phones on me. They should last me a little while and allow me to keep in contact with Isabelle and anyone else that I might need.

Despite all of my preparation, I still haven't figured everything out. I thought that everything was under control and had a process for how to proceed.

A plan allows you to act without thinking so that your actions are not muddled by worry. Uncertainty and anxiety cause us to make mistakes and, in this case, I can't allow for any. But the thing is that in my preparations I always assumed that I would be running away on my own.

I have another passport and the best thing would be to head to the airport and fly away to some country without extradition before the cops are even on my trail.

Perhaps that's still the best decision and yet that's not the one that I'm making. Instead, I'm headed back to Pennsylvania to the place where I was held captive for two crimes that I did not commit.

These thoughts keep circling around in my head for hours. I get to Spokane and then to Idaho. I cross over to Montana and still I'm not sure that this is the best plan of action.

Perhaps what I should do is to simply fly somewhere safe and then reach out to Isabelle and ask her to meet me.

No one is on her trail. No one knows that we are together.

Still, I drive east.

I call her a few times on the burner phone, but she doesn't answer. I text and tell her to reach me here, but again she doesn't respond. It's too late for her to be at work, but she might be sleeping. The fact that she is so sick from the pregnancy is not helping matters.

Flying out together will be harder, but it might also make me seem less suspicious.

There are couples flying out all the time and if anyone does look for me, they'll be looking for someone traveling solo.

I drive straight through the night, occasionally texting her, but avoiding any more phone calls in case she's sleeping. When I get to South Dakota, I stop wrestling with myself about my decision to leave and head to her house.

There's no point in second-guessing myself anymore. This is something that I've done and there are benefits to traveling with Isabelle as well.

For one, she's really sick and I'm not sure if she'll be able to get on the plane by herself. The other is that we can make this decision together, in person.

This affects her as much as it affects me and it has a great effect on our life together. Everything is fine now.

No authorities are looking for me.

The Elliott brothers are not going to tell anyone that they have extorted me because they'd rather just keep the $19 million.

I have not put up a fight and I am sure that their attorney has already notified them that I have sent over the paperwork.

Around Chicago, it suddenly occurs to me that my situation is a little bit safer than I had previously thought. If the Elliott brothers do end up going to the authorities and telling them about me then I will of course tell them that they have not repaid me the $19 million they owe me.

They have extorted me and they're going to pay for that extortion even if I have to spend the rest of my life in prison trying to prove that.

Of course, I won't see a dime of that money, but I'll make a lot of trouble for them and they know it.

Realizing this makes me feel a little bit better. Perhaps my situation is not as dire as I had thought. Perhaps there is still a good chance that I might get away after all.

Dawn settles in and sunlight starts to peek over the horizon in my rearview mirror. It's a new day and I have been driving for hours with barely any breaks.

I know that I need a nap, but I don't feel safe taking one. Not yet.

My eyelids are heavy. I won't be able to hold on for much longer. All of the cups of coffee that I have consumed have stopped working along with the 5-hour Energy drinks.

Luckily, a few miles down the road I see a rest area with a bunch of eighteen-wheelers lined up. This is where people rest and it will be easy to blend in.

I pull over, grab a spot in the parking lot, and start to recline my seat. I fall into a deep asleep before I lay all the way down.

18

ISABELLE

I feel sick the following morning, but my weakness and nausea are little bit better. The medication is definitely working.

It's still very hard for me to get out of bed and to move my head from side to side without getting dizzy, but I'm starting to figure out what to do.

I have talked to Tyler a few times since he got the decision and I got the sense that he is at peace with it. It's not something that he wasn't expecting and the last time we spoke, he seemed to be looking forward to starting a new chapter in his life.

Of course, the fact that I'm pregnant has overshadowed a lot of what had happened at the hearing.

The more days that pass, the easier it becomes to accept the fact that I'm pregnant.

At first, it was such a surprise. It completely shocked me, actually scared me.

I have spent so much of my life worrying about possibly getting pregnant and using all sorts of precautions to prevent that from happening that it feels almost unnatural to be happy about being pregnant.

Of course, that's not the case.

I'm in a solid relationship. I love Tyler and he loves me. We want to spend the rest of our lives together.

The only thing that made me feel uncomfortable about it was the fact that he has his past, the secret identity, and this thing that can ruin everything, but he has promised to deal with that.

I told him that I would help. We discussed the Mallory Deals podcast and the website. I am also compiling a list of all of the other people on the Internet that believe that he's innocent. They are a great starting point, but they're also only that, a starting point.

It will take a lot of work to sway public opinion, but that's something that we will have to do, even if we do it from afar.

Of course, for that, we will need an attorney.

I haven't given much thought to hiring one, but when everything comes down and I start to feel a little better, that's something that I intend to talk to Tyler about.

We need someone good.

Someone we can trust.

We would also have to take precautions.

Untraceable phone.

Undisclosed location.

Maybe even no knowledge about his new name.

I'm not really sure how it works or how it should work. All I know is that I intend to protect the father of my child to the best of my ability if it's the last thing I do.

As all of these thoughts swirl around in my mind, I force myself to my feet and start to feel dizzy again.

Lying on my back is one thing, but there's something that is completely unnatural and impossible about standing up and walking around. At least for now.

Still, I need to pee and for that, I need to go to the bathroom. It's not far, it's attached to the master bedroom, and yet by the time I get there I feel like I both need to have a bowel movement and throw up at the same time, only I don't know which one to do first.

I try to hold it in and then bend myself over the toilet, gagging. I force my fingers down my throat to try to hurry the process along, but only a little bit comes out.

I feel a bit better.

I let out a sigh of relief and quickly pull down my pants and sit down.

One wave of relief follows another as I double over and bury my head between my knees. After a few moments, I finally feel okay.

By the time I stand up and wash my hands, the nausea comes back.

It has something to do with being upright, standing on two feet. I force myself to go to the kitchen while I have the strength and make myself something to eat.

This moment of feeling somewhat okay right after throwing up, lasts only a brief period of time and unfortunately, Tyler isn't here to help me make toast, which is the only food that seems to quell this thing.

I check in the pantry and luckily there's a loaf of bread that I had forgotten about. It's already sliced and I throw some with oil on it in the pan. While it browns, I look down to my phone and text Tyler. I had tried to call him earlier today a number of times, but all I got back was a cryptic text that says that he can't talk now. And then nothing.

I know that he probably needs some space. He still has to figure out some things with his business, probably clear out his office, and say goodbye to everyone.

I can't imagine how difficult this process is, but I would be lying if I didn't say that a part of me was a little glad that this happened the way that it happened. It's not that I would have minded moving to Seattle, probably not, but it's more that his heart didn't really seem into it.

Maybe it was at one point, when he was trying to build something or start something to take his mind off of me and us, but things are different now. I know that he wants to spend a lot of time with me and the baby. He would not be able to do that if he were still running that large property and making all those changes all by himself.

Just as I pop the toast onto a plate, my doorbell rings.

Who could that be?

I never have anyone just pop by, but it might be a neighbor in need of some help.

I walk to the door and peek through the glass. There are two police officers standing on my porch.

My heart drops, but I force myself to stay calm.

"There's nothing to worry about," I say to myself silently. "Everything is going to be okay. They don't know anything."

The pep talk helps, but only a little bit.

"Hello," I say, opening the door.

"Are you Isabelle Nesbitt?"

"Yes I am. How can I help you?"

One of the officer's inches forward as if he expects me to invite him in, but, of course, I don't.

"Ms. Nesbitt, we have some questions that we need to ask you."

"Okay…" I say slowly.

"Would you mind accompanying us to the precinct?"

All the blood drains away from my face. I swallow hard and almost cough because my mouth is so parched.

"I'm sorry, what is this about?" I ask, crossing my arms.

I see my reflection in the sunglasses of the one cop who looks a little bit familiar. My arms are folded across my chest and I look like I am holding myself.

I'm dressed in unmatched pajamas, loose and ill fitting. My hair is dirty and untamed. My face is make-up free and almost greenish in color.

I take a deep breath and straighten my shoulders, trying to infuse myself with confidence.

When the one on the left takes off his sunglasses, I immediately recognize him as the cop who stopped me when they had barricaded the street looking for Tyler.

Does this have anything to do with *that*?

He's wearing a nameplate: Walter McVay. That's right, now I remember. It reminded me of the Oklahoma City bombing guy.

"I'm not really sure what you want to talk to me about, but I'm not feeling too well," I say.

I debate whether I should tell them that I'm pregnant.

For now, I decide to just go with the flu and perhaps I can pull out that card later if needed.

The taller guy next to McVay takes a step closer to me and kneels down. I look up at him, feeling him trying to impose himself on me.

"This is very important, Miss. We really need your help with something and since this is a very delicate matter, it would be best dealt with at the precinct."

I know that I should say no and to please contact my lawyer, but it also feels very suspicious to do that. I don't know what they have or don't have. I definitely feel the pressure to cave in.

“Listen, I'd love to help you,” I say, taking a deep breath and hoping to God that I don't start to feel lightheaded again. “I can’t go to the precinct right now. I'm not feeling well.”

I touch my stomach, but don't elaborate.

“You really need to come with us ma'am,” McVay says and there is something in his eyes.

“Or what?”

This seems to catch them by surprise. They shake their heads and exchange looks. I hold my hand in a fist behind me, pressing my fingers hard into the soft part of my palm.

I am interested in knowing what they know and what they want to ask me, but their presence here can only be something bad. I don't intend on telling them anything and the best way to do that is to not go along with what they want.

"I don't know why you can't just ask me what you want to ask me right here?" I say. "If not then I'm just going to go."

I wait by the door, but one of them pushes it open.

I realize suddenly that there are two of them. They're both men and they are armed. Cops have done a lot worse to people who they have suspected of a lot less. Fear runs through my veins, but I remain steadfast

"Am I under arrest for something?"

"No." McVeigh said. "You do not want to be doing this. You want to cooperate with us. It's in your best interest."

"I happen to know that it's in people's best interests to speak to an attorney when they have cops on their doorstep talking to them in this manner," I say slowly, but sternly. "If I'm not under arrest, then I don't want to talk to you, but I will get an attorney that you can speak to instead."

I close the door in their faces and my body begins to tremble. Did I just do that? Did that actually happen?

I lean against the wall and slow down my breathing, intentionally inhaling very slowly and exhaling even slower through my nose. After a few moments, my heartbeat slows down, but my anxiety continues to skyrocket.

They wouldn't be here if it weren't serious and I don't know what it is. I don't know what they want. The thing is that by not coming with them, I only made it more suspicious.

It's so easy to sit on your couch and judge someone for going with the police to the precinct and making a statement when you really should not, but the problem is what happens when you do not.

They already suspect me of something. They would not be here if they didn't.

Did I just make everything worse?

I open my eyes and look out the door. That's when I see his face. Leaning in and glaring through the window, I jump back. My chest tightens.

It's the same cop from before, but it's really the expression on his face that takes me by surprise. He smiles from ear to ear, almost gleeful.

I watch him raise his finger and ring my doorbell. I don't want to answer, so I just remain motionless against the wall. The problem is that they know that I'm here. They can see me and I can't leave.

"Open the door, Isabelle," Officer McVay yells.

He uses something metal to knock on the outside of the door, creating a loud clinking sound that sends cold sweat down my spine.

"We need to talk to you!"

It requires actual effort to make my feet work and bring my body back to the front door. Eventually I manage. They continue to knock. It becomes more and more menacing.

"You are going to have to come with us, ma'am," the other cop says.

"Am I under arrest?" I ask calmly but with as much authority as I can muster.

"Not yet," McVay threatens.

"If you don't come with us to the precinct and answer our questions," the other cop says, throwing his hands up, "we will have to arrest you on obstructing an official investigation. I really hope that we don't have to do that."

We dance around the circle for some time but eventually I give in. It is clear to me that they won't let this go and I have to make some sort of official statement.

I intend to take my car, but they insist on driving me over themselves.

It is not lost on me that I have to sit in the back of the police car. The doors lock on the outside and there are no doorknobs. I can't open the window and my only saving grace is that I'm not handcuffed.

They don't say anything on the fifteen minute drive and I don't either. Instead, I use this time to organize my thoughts.

Of course, I'm scared. More like terrified, but I can't let them use that against me. I don't know what they have, but I'm not going to give them anymore.

Even though I didn't have much of a choice about coming here, I do have a choice as to what I'm going to say and what I do not say. They can make threats about me obstructing their investigation as much as they want, but they can't make me talk.

I don't know how long they can hold me, but I hope that they give me access to the bathroom because I know that I'm going to need it.

On the drive over, I start to feel queasy again. Even though I make all of these decisions about how I'm going to get through this, as soon as the nausea since then, nothing makes sense anymore.

"I'm starting to feel sick to my stomach," I say, feeling the blood drain away from my face.

We go over one bump and then another. When we drive over a pothole, the bile in the pit of my stomach rises up my esophagus.

"I don't know if you think I'm kidding, but I'm not," I mumble.

"What are you talking about?"

"I'm nauseous," I say, shaking my head, bending it in between my legs. "I'm going to get sick."

"You better not throw up in my car," one yells, but it's too late. I open my mouth and it all comes out, all over the back of his seat.

"I really don't feel good," I mumble. "Do you have any tissues?"

The two of them up front start to argue, but I can't make sense out of anything that they're saying. Suddenly, the car makes a quick right turn and this triggers another wave of nausea.

Somehow, I end up in a nondescript empty room somewhere in the hallways of the precinct. The room looks exactly like it does in all of those interrogation videos that you have seen on television. A simple desk, two chairs, and a camera mounted on the ceiling.

"I need to go to the bathroom," I say, putting my head down on the table.

The lights are too bright and fluorescent, giving me a pounding headache at the front of my head.

"I don't know," McVay hesitates, but another officer comes over and escorts me to the women's restroom.

I see the officer's feet through the underneath part of the stall while I try to decide whether I should first throw up or sit down on the toilet and deal with diarrhea.

She's waiting by the sink, facing away from me, giving me the illusion of privacy

"I don't know why I am here," I say.

"Ma'am, I'm really just here to escort you here and take you back to the room. I can't ask you any questions."

"Good, because I don't have any answers," I mumble. "I do want you to help me with something."

"Ma'am, I'm really not in the position–" she says

"I need to speak to an attorney. I don't know why those officers brought me here, but I am not going to be making any statements until I have legal counsel."

Silence falls.

She doesn't respond and I know that I have spoken the magic words. Of course they can stall and they can protest probably trying to convince me otherwise, but I tried to be as clear as possible to make my case.

"I'm serious," I say, clearing my throat. "I'm not going to talk to anybody until my attorney is here."

19

ISABELLE

The problem, of course, is that I don't have an attorney. Luckily, I have my phone and my purse on me so I look up names of people. I have no idea how this works. Do I just call the office and asked him to come in?

I flush the toilet and come out to wash my hands.

The female officer standing next to me is about my age with her hair pinned tightly in a bun. She's wearing minimal makeup and her nails are cut short with a little bit of nail polish for shine. Her olive skin and her almond shaped eyes make it difficult to identify her ethnicity, but I have no doubt that in this precinct, she's an outsider and will be one for a long time.

She shows me back to the room and tells McVay what I said. He's less than pleased and isn't afraid to show me.

"You know, when I first came over to your house, I had my doubts about your involvement in this. I thought that a nice girl like you would have nothing to do with someone like Tyler McDermott but given your actions out here and how you refuse to answer any of our questions, I'm starting to have my doubts."

So, this is about Tyler, I say to myself, but I don't betray anything to him.

Instead I sit back in the chair and give him a slight nod.

"So, you're really not going to say anything?" he pushes me. "Do you want to know who Tyler is? Do you want to know why we want to talk to you?"

"Yes, I do, but I also know how dangerous it can be for people to talk to police officers."

"It's not dangerous at all if you have nothing to hide."

"Yeah, I'm not so sure," I say, shaking my head. "In fact, I know that there are plenty of innocent people locked up in prisons all over America that would agree with me."

"Listen, you have nothing to worry about, Isabelle," McVay says, leaning closer to me. "We can protect you. We are on your side. We just want to know what happened."

I give him a moment and then shake my head again.

"I'm not going to talk to you about anything without a lawyer."

I REACH FOR MY PHONE, but he stops me.

"I'm just going to try to find an attorney."

"No," he says, shaking his head. "This doesn't work this way."

"What are you talking about?"

He takes my purse and phone away from me and goes outside.

Keenly aware of the fact that I'm being filmed, I try to stay calm, but inside, my heart is pounding out of my chest.

What the hell do I do?

How is this happening?

A few minutes later, he returns and hands me the phone book.

I've seen them dropped off on people's curbs, but I haven't actually used one in years. In fact, I wonder why they are still being printed.

"I need to use my phone," I say. "I don't know any of these lawyers."

"That's your problem," McVeigh says. "You can call want if you want, but I'm not here to make things easier for you if you're not willing to make things easier for me."

"Can I have my phone back at least?"

He stares at me, as if he's debating whether or not to let me use it. After a moment, he gives in.

"No searching. No Google. You only use it to make a call. I'm watching you."

In the phone book I look under a for attorneys. It refers me to L for law firms and that's when I find two pages of names. There are a few advertisements and pictures, but nothing else.

How am I supposed to decide who is the best person for me?

I glance over at McVay who seems awfully satisfied and pleased with himself. He knows that he's getting something on me and he likes that.

I turn my attention back to the phone book, trying to keep my nerves to myself so that he doesn't see exactly how flustered I am.

I scan the names again and at the top I see his name: Mallory Deals. There's no About section. There is no picture. There's just a phone number.

I swallow hard. I might as well call him. As soon as I start to dial the number, someone comes in and pulls McVay out of the room.

I guess I could easily Google one of the other attorneys now, but there's really only one person who I want to help me.

"Hello?" a man says and I recognize his voice from the podcast.

"Mr. Deals? My name is Isabelle Nesbitt and I need your help." I can hear the hesitation in my voice, but there isn't much that I can do about it.

I'm trying to collect my thoughts and figure out how to tell him that I need help without revealing too much.

They probably left because all communications between the client and attorney have to be private, but that doesn't mean they're not currently recording me. I have to assume that they are.

"I'm sorry, but I'm not taking on any new clients at this point," he says rather dismissively.

"Mr. Deals, please, they have me at the station. You're the only one who can help me."

"I highly doubt that," he says, clearing his throat.

This isn't going well. It feels like he's just about to hang up on me and I have to do something to stop him.

"Mr. Deals, this has to do with Tyler McDermott," I say quietly.

"Excuse me?" he asks after a moment.

"You heard me. Please. I need an attorney."

"Don't say a word," he instructs. "Give me the address and I'll be there soon as I can."

I hang up the phone and stare at the screen. It goes black and I wait for McVay or another police officer to come in, but no one does. I sit back in the chair, but it's hard plastic and extremely uncomfortable.

They have offered me some coffee or a soda, but I have declined and now I wish that I hadn't.

The room is blank, completely devoid of character, and that's probably its purpose. It's supposed to make you think. Make you wonder about what they have on you and how many years you are going to spend in more rooms like this if you don't tell them the truth.

I haven't heard from Tyler yet even though I tried to call him a number of times. I hope to God that he doesn't call me here and I'm grateful that I didn't program my phone with his name in the contact information.

Minutes pass slowly here.

I stare at the wall for a long time. I'm tempted to look at my phone, but I don't want them to take it away from me so I don't want to draw any unnecessary attention to it. I don't know exactly how a lot of legal things work.

Would they be able to look at my chat log from the time that I was here if they suspect that I'm in contact with someone?

How much access to my private things do they have?

I know that they need probable cause, but what exactly constitutes probable cause?

An hour later, there's a knock on the door and Deals comes in. He's taller than I thought he would be with striking cheekbones and a no-nonsense expression on his face. He shakes my hand and introduces himself, narrowing his eyes, probably trying to figure out how I fit into the case.

"What have you told them?" he asks.

"Nothing. I don't really even know what this is about, but I know it's best to have an attorney here."

He gives me a slight nod and then invites the cops inside. When the door swings open, I see *her*.

She walks down the hallway, turning to look at me over her shoulder. My heart drops.

It's Libby.

Her shoulders are slumped down and she looks guilty, like she has done something that she should not have.

Why is she here?

What has she told them?

My head starts to buzz as it hits me that she knows all about me and Tyler.

I trusted her and the only reason why she would be here is if she had turned me in.

I take a string of small breaths trying to get some oxygen into my chest, but it just makes the pain worse.

I blink over and over again trying to keep my tears at bay. I swallow hard and ask for some water. Someone walks out to get me a cup and then comes back in. I drink all of it in one swift gulp, but it barely quenches my thirst.

I glance over at Deals and see his lips moving. McVay positions himself across from us, saying something. My head is pounding so hard that it's almost as if they are talking in another room. All I hear is the multiple of their voices, but I can't understand a single word.

I force myself to focus and slowly things start to make more sense.

Deals and McVay have been discussing the rules of the questions they can ask. I still don't know the content of the questions. I can tell he's trying to protect me.

"Okay, how about this?" McVay asks. "I ask the questions and you either answer them or don't answer them. Does that work?"

Deals looks at me and I give him a slight nod.

"Do you know who Tyler McDermott is?" McVeigh asks.

"Yes," I say quietly, knowing that I can't deny knowing of him.

"How do you know him?"

"I have seen his pictures on the news and you showed me his Wanted poster when you were looking for him in the area."

"Okay, but do you also know him from before?"

I debate whether I should admit the fact that we went to school together, but I finally give in. That's an easy thing to check and there are other people that knew that we were good friends.

"I was friends with him in middle school," I finally say.

"Have you seen him since?"

"You mean besides on the news?"

"Yes. In person."

"No," I say sternly and with as much confidence as possible. "Absolutely not."

"Are you sure?"

I look over at Deals. This is where I need his help.

"My client has already told you that she has not seen him. Asking her the question in a different way is not going to change the answer."

"We'll see about that," he says under his breath. "So, you have never had any contact with him at all?"

I'm about to open my mouth when Deals stops me.

"Listen, if you're just here to pressure her, then I'm going to instruct my client not to answer any more of your questions. She's told you no twice now. I'm sorry if that's inconvenient for your case, but if you have any other questions, we can just move this along."

I expect to stay at the station for a few more hours, answering their questions through my teeth, but much to my surprise, the interview comes to a swift end.

I remain steadfast in the fact that I have not been in contact with Tyler at all and nothing they say makes me budge.

After a little while, they go out into the hallway along with Deals.

When he comes back in a few minutes later, he tells me that I'm free to go and I follow him out to the parking lot.

"You better not leave the jurisdiction. We're not done here," McVay threatens.

Outside the building, I let out a sigh of relief, but I know that I'm not totally off the hook.

Libby is there.

I saw her and the only reason why she would be here is me.

“What happened? What is happening?” I ask.

Deals pulls out a piece of paper from his briefcase and hands it to me. It's a contract, giving him permission to officially represent me. I can't sign it fast enough and when I do, he says, they suspect that I’m involved with Tyler.

My mouth drops open and I ask, “Why?”

He looks around. “Are you in contact with him?”

I shake my head. He tilts his, not believing me.

“You have to tell me the truth, Isabelle. I'm your attorney now. Everything you say to me we will keep in confidence, but I can't represent you if I don't know what's going on.”

“I can't tell you here,” I say, shaking my head and looking at the police station looming in the distance. We are just in the parking lot and I'm afraid that they have ears everywhere.

He points to his car, urging me to get in.

“Will you give me a ride home?” I ask. “They drove me here, otherwise I'll have to get a cab.”

"Of course. It will give us time to talk."

I get in his car and give him my address, which he puts into the GPS on his phone.

When we pull out of the parking lot, he tells me that they think that I'm having a relationship with Tyler.

I don't know what to say so I just stare out of the window. I want to trust him. I want to tell him the truth, but I just met him and I don't know if I can.

"Why do they think that?" I ask.

"They had someone make a report. I think you saw her in the there. She's a friend of yours?"

"How did you know?" I ask, my face growing pale.

"I'm very observant."

"Do you think the cops noticed?"

"They brought you there on purpose. To get you to talk. They know something, but they don't know everything."

"I can't believe that she would do that. I thought she was my friend."

"You told her about Tyler? Did he come to see you after he escaped?"

I shake my head and turn my face toward the river.

Suddenly, the car jerks and pulls over. Deals puts the car into park and then turns to face me.

"You have to tell me the truth, Isabelle. I can't help you with anything if I have both of my hands tied behind my back. I have to know what's going on."

I nod. I know that he's right, but I have already told the truth to one person and it all came back on me.

"You called me for a reason. Why? Did you see my website? Do you know about my podcast?"

"You seemed to be the only person that believes that he's innocent."

"That's right. I know that he is."

"How?"

"The prosecutor is hiding DNA evidence. He hasn't had it tested because he knows that it will prove that there is somebody else's DNA at the crime scene. The real killers."

"Why? Why are they doing this to Tyler?"

"He's an easy target. Most of the time it's the husband. She was cheating on him so they have motive, but he didn't do it. He has an alibi that he's keeping secret."

"That's exactly right," I say, leaning back in my seat. "How do *you* know this?"

"I have my hunches. I have read the transcript and there are a few places in there where he mentions something along those lines, but then doesn't elaborate. He is keeping something secret. I've been in this business long enough to know that. So, tell me, what happened? What does Libby know?" Deals asks.

I shake my head again. I still don't really trust him, but I don't have much of a choice.

"Listen, the cops know everything that she knows, So you better tell me so that I'm prepared to talk to them. I don't know how involved you are in any of this and I'll do my best to defend you against anything they may bring up. This is serious. They're looking for him. It has been a while, but this is how they're going to catch him."

"What do you mean?"

"After some time passes, people start to feel safe. They let their guard down. They're not as careful. That's when they start to make mistakes and that's when the FBI and the cops get their way."

I nod my head. I know exactly what he means. I realize that the only way out of this is to tell him what I know and what Libby told the police.

20

ISABELLE

After Deals drops me off at home, I go straight to the bathroom and throw up. Somehow, my nausea has been kept at bay this whole time, but as soon as I get home, it overwhelms me.

I take some Tylenol for the pounding headache and sit down on the couch to try to figure out how everything has turned out the way that it has.

On the drive over here, I told Deals most of the details. I told him everything, but I kept some information about his present life and whereabouts to myself.

He told me that he's going to think about the best way to approach this thing and that he will be in touch tonight or tomorrow at the latest.

Cradling my phone in my lap, I fight the urge to call Tyler. I haven't discussed this with Deals, but I know that cops can tap phones.

They suspect that I am in contact with him and I know that the worst thing that I can do is to reach out. But I have to warn him. He has to know that they are looking at me and he needs to stay away.

I'm not particularly hungry, so I go to the kitchen and make myself something to drink.

I pop another Diclegis pill to keep the nausea down, but by the time the sun starts to set, I start to feel weak and exhausted again. This is usually how I start to feel at this time of day. That's why I started cooking early, so I can have something to nibble on throughout the evening.

Just as I get settled into my recliner and turn on the television, there's a knock on the door. I don't want to answer. I don't want to talk to anybody, but the knock is persistent. I force myself to look over the couch and see her silhouette peeking through the window.

It's Libby.

"Isabelle, open the door," she yells. "I have to talk to you!"

"Go away!" I scream back.

I turn the television up louder to try to drown her out, hoping that she takes the hint, but she doesn't.

She continues to knock and knock. When the knocking finally stops, I let out a sigh of relief, but then I suddenly see her on my porch.

The sliding door leading into my kitchen is unlocked and she lets herself in.

"What are you doing? Why are you here?"

"I have to talk to you, please. You have to know that I did not turn you in. You have to believe me." She's frantic and out-of-control.

I shake my head. I don't want to believe her.

"Isabelle, please. Everything they learned, they found out from Darren."

I shake my head, no. I don't believe her. How would Darren know about any of this?

"I have no idea what you're talking about," I say.

I feel sucked into this conversation, but I want to be careful. I can't confirm or deny anything.

What if she is wired?

What if she is just talking to me to get me to say something on a recording?

I point to her clothes. She furrows her brows. I point again. I am not going to say the words out loud.

She still doesn't get it.

Are you wearing a wire? I mouth the words, gesturing to her.

"No, absolutely not!"

I shake my head, refusing to believe her.

To prove her point, she begins to undress.

She takes everything off except for her underwear and I look around carefully checking for wire.

I even check her ears for tiny listening aids, but I find nothing. Then I check her hair.

"Okay, get dressed," I say.

After she puts everything back on, I pull on my boots.

"What are you doing?" she asks.

"Let's go on a walk."

I lead Libby away from the house down the empty street illuminated by tall streetlights. A car drives by. A garage door opens and the car drives inside. There are a few cars parked on the street, since almost everyone parks in their garages.

My neighbor and I exchange a brief wave of hello, and I wait until she pulls inside before saying a word.

"Why are you here?" I ask after we reach the end of the street and turn right.

"I'm really sorry. I came here to apologize."

"You have nothing to apologize for."

"Of course, I do," Libby says. "Those cops came to talk to you because of *me*. Because of what happened at my house."

Of course I want to know what happened, but my mind goes in circles.

What if this is a setup? She's not wearing a wire and, of course, I can't deny it, but what if it still somehow is set up?

I walk further away from the house and take a careful look back and forth. There's no one around. She's not wearing any sort of recording device. I should feel safe.

"What are we doing here?" Libby asks.

"You know exactly what. I don't know if my house is bugged."

She stares at me. I turn away from her and continue to walk at a steady pace. After a few moments, she catches up with me.

"I have to tell you what happened."

"Go ahead."

"It was Darren. He's the one that called the police. Carolyn had overheard us talking. She said something to him. He questioned her and she told him everything."

I shrug, keeping my surprise completely to myself.

"We shouldn't have talked in front of the kids, but I'm here to tell you that I had nothing to do with turning you in. I never told him a word. When he confronted me about it, I denied it all."

I continue to walk, but she grabs onto my hand and spins me around.

"You have to believe me, Isabelle. Do you know how hard it is for me to tell my daughter that she did not hear what she thought she did?"

I shake my head. I swallow hard. As much as I don't want to talk about this in case anyone is listening, she's also my friend and she's in pain.

"Okay," I say slowly. "I believe you."

She looks up at me and I take her hand in mine. I pull her close and give her a warm hug. She sobs into my shoulder and I start to cry as well.

"What did you tell them?"

"Nothing," I say, shaking my head. "I got an attorney. I didn't tell them anything because there's nothing to tell."

She looks at me, surprised, but then I give her a wink. She nods like she understands.

"I can't talk about any of this," I say. "On my attorney's advice. Whatever Carolyn heard, it's not true."

She looks at me and again I give her a wink.

It's the only thing that I can permit myself at this point. We are in the darkness, but I have seen enough shows on television to know that this is how the police will get me and even worse than that, this is how the police will find Tyler.

That thought makes my skin crawl. Tyler.

I still haven't gotten in touch with him. He has no idea what's going on and I can't call him on my phone.

At this point, I have to assume that my house is bugged and my phone is tapped.

How do I warn him?

"What can I do?" Libby asks. She looks at me with her big wide eyes and I know that this is my chance.

I need to warn him. This is what I need to tell her, but I'm afraid to say the words out loud. Yet, this isn't exactly the kind of thing that I can convey in a look or an expression.

After careful consideration, I decide to take a chance. She's not wired and no one can be tracking what we're saying out here, outside of the house. At least I hope not.

"I need a phone," I say in a barely audible whisper.

She nods very slowly and asks, "Do you want to use mine?"

"No."

"You want to get a disposable one?"

"Can you get me one?" I whisper.

She nods.

We get back to her car and when she starts it, I put my finger up to her mouth. I want to talk about this, but I'm not going to do it here. Instead, I turn up the music.

"You could get into a lot of trouble for helping me," I say when we walk across the parking lot to Walmart.

"I know, but I have to do it anyway. I love you and you have been a wonderful friend to me this whole time. Darren should not have done that. He should have talked to me first. I'm so sorry that he's messed everything up."

"Thank you," I say. "I really appreciate that."

In addition to the disposable phone, I pick up a few magazines and a book as well as some earphones. I figured this way it would look less suspicious if anyone were to look at a tape of this later on.

Am I really already making plans for what's going to happen when this goes to trial? Another bead of sweat runs down my back, but I ignore it.

Libby pays for everything and I throw in a pack of M&Ms as we stand in line. I promise to pay her back, again in a barely audible whisper.

As soon as we are outside, I want to grab the phone away from her and call him, but there are cameras out here and I have to be careful.

I get in the car with her and we drive to a local park. There, I get out and dial the number that I have memorized a long time ago.

He doesn't answer. I don't know what to do. I want to leave a message, but I don't want my voice recorded.

I want to text him, but again I don't want the record of it.

I call again and again, but he still doesn't answer. I decide to go with the voicemail. That way he'll know for sure since I'm calling from a different number.

"It's me," I say, my voice clearly rattled. "Something has happened. Please don't call me or visit me here. You need to go. You need to run away. You can't help me and I hope being in contact doesn't make everything worse. I'll do my best to protect you. I love you always."

Tears are streaming down my face when I say the last sentence.

When I get back to the car, I decide to hold onto the phone in case he calls me back.

21

TYLER

It takes me many hours on the road to get to Isabelle's home in Pittsburgh where it all started. Pulling into her development, I suddenly have a flashback of lying in the back of her trunk as she drove out of here in the dead of night.

Rain falls in sheets and my wipers are working overtime. I still haven't ditched the car or gotten a new one. My only saving grace is that the Elliott brothers have not notified the authorities but instead decided to take me up on keeping the nineteen million that they have no right to keep.

I don't have a plan. I thought I would get one when I got here, but that's far from the truth.

All of these hours of driving and I'm still not sure what to do. I have to run away and start a new life again, but I can't do that without Isabelle. When I get to her neighborhood, I park the car a few blocks away. There are not that many cars that park on her street and mine will undoubtedly stand out.

I'm dressed like a runner in a pair of dark sweatpants and a hoodie. I put the ski cap over my eyes and try to look as inconspicuous as possible. I decide that I'm going to sneak in through her back yard. Hopefully, she will let me in through her sliding door into her kitchen.

As soon as I am about to turn onto her street, I see four police cars with their lights on parked right out front of her house.

The doors swing open and they rush up to her porch.

My heart drops. I don't know what to.

I slow down to barely a jog, to buy myself some time, and all I hear is someone yell, “It's the police! Open the door!”

A moment later they slam through the door and rush into her house.

22

ISABELLE

They burst through my door. They knock first, identify themselves, but then they're inside.

As soon as I reach for the handle, they rush past me, looking for him everywhere. Two deputies in uniform prowl around my house, their guns drawn, supporting their hands with flashlights.

"What are you doing here? What's going on?" I ask, trying to be as surefooted and confident as possible.

I stand in a wide stance and cross my arms in front of me, but inside I'm trembling.

"Where is he?" the bigger one, with the receding hairline, snaps.

"Who?"

"You know who, Tyler McDermott."

"I don't know what you're talking about," I say.

Libby and I exchange a glance and I know her well enough to know that she's terrified, but trying to hold on, just like I am.

"Where's your phone?" the skinnier one asks, pointing the flashlight into my eyes and blinding me.

"Sorry," he adds in a casual tone, as if it were an accident, but both of us know that it wasn't.

"I don't know what you're talking about, but can you please leave?" I say.

"He's hiding out here, isn't he? You're protecting him."

"You have just searched my whole house," I say. "You were in the garage. You were in the bedrooms."

"Where is he?" They don't give up.

"I haven't seen him in a long time," I say, being vague on purpose because I don't want to be caught in a lie.

"Where did you two go?" the skinnier one asks. "Why did you leave the house?"

And suddenly it hits me.

"Are you following me?" I ask.

I walk over to the window and look out at their car. It's unmarked. It looks familiar.

"You were *following* me." I point my finger at the older one, who looks a little annoyed by this assignment and not particularly interested in being here.

"Listen, we all know what you did," he says. "You went to Walmart, you got a phone so you could call him. We're going to catch you in this lie and then you're going to be in big trouble."

"I don't know what you're talking about," I say quickly, but calmly. I had to get the words out before the tremble that has taken over my hands rushes up to my mouth. "I need you to leave."

"Show me your phone." He doesn't let up.

"No, I don't have to do that."

"Yes, you do. I'm a police officer."

"Without a warrant!" I snap. "Even if I had a phone, I wouldn't show you one without a search warrant. Are you here to arrest me?" I catch him hesitating. "Then leave, you're trespassing."

When I shut the door behind them, Libby stares at me.

"I've never seen you like that," she adds.

This is the first time that she has said a word since they had rushed into the house, and I'm glad for it. If she had spoken earlier, they would've known for sure they were onto something.

"I've never seen you like that, so confident and firm," she says.

"Well, I had to get a little tougher."

"I'll say." Libby goes over to the couch, sitting down on the edge of the cushion. She puts her purse on her lap and just stares into space.

"Can I get you something to drink?" I ask.

She shakes her head no at first, but then relents. "Tea would be nice."

"I could use a vodka," I joke.

She smiles. "Me, too."

"Unfortunately, I don't have any."

“Black tea's fine." She waves in my general direction, still clutching onto her purse.

"I'm sorry that I put you in the middle of all of this," I say, pouring the hot water into two identical mugs.

I drop a teabag into each one and resist the urge to reuse it. I don't like mine soaking in there too long and becoming tart to the taste, but I know that she likes hers dark.

"I can't believe that you talked to the cops like that," she says, finally letting go of her purse, dropping it to the carpet and bringing the mug to her lips. "I could never do that."

"Yes, you could.” I nod. "It's easy. You get used to it after a while. I'm just sorry that this whole thing happened."

"I shouldn't have said anything to *him*."

I don't know why she avoided saying her husband's name, but I accept her apology.

"Listen, it doesn't matter. I mean, it's not that it doesn't matter, but I appreciate you making it up to me, coming here and helping me out with the phone."

"For whatever good it did," she adds.

"Yeah, but I had to try, you know?"

"What do we do now?" she asks, taking another big sip, even though the water is steaming hot.

"I'm not sure," I whisper. "If I can't get in touch with him, I don't know."

"And what about the baby?" Libby asks.

I look down at my stomach. "I've done a lot of stuff on my own, so maybe this is just one of those things."

"No, it's hard, but it's not just that. Of course you can do it, but Tyler's the father. He needs to be part of this."

"He's running away for his life. I can't ask him to endanger himself and ... I don't know. I don't know what I'm saying," I whisper.

This is the first time that I have talked about it or even let myself think about the possibility of raising our child on my own.

"Are you happy about the baby, outside of whatever's going on with Tyler?"

I shrug. "It's hard for me to say. I was never one of those women that just desperately wanted to have a child. A pet, yes, a dog, but this? I don't know. Maybe it's because I've had so much drama with my mom and I just didn't want any extra entanglements. But now that I'm pregnant, it would be easier to be happy about this, like really, really happy, if I didn't feel so nauseous all the time. But overall, yes, I would say I am glad."

"You are?" Her face lights up.

"Yeah, now that it's here," I say, putting my hand over my stomach. "I don't know. I was starting to imagine the life that I could have, the mom that I could be, the child that I could raise, and it's nice. They're all nice thoughts."

"You're going to be a great mom," Libby says, draping her arm around my shoulder.

We stay here for a few moments, and I remember what it was like when I was little and how we have been through so much and how, in life, sometimes there's still so much more to go.

Libby stays for close to an hour, even though she keeps mentioning the fact that she has to go. I don't think she wants to leave me, and I don't want her to leave. Today was incredibly stressful, and I have no idea what tomorrow will bring.

When she can't stall much longer, she excuses herself to use the bathroom and then runs back toward me almost immediately.

"Somebody's here," she whispers under her breath, pointing to my guest room. She looks terrified and her face has turned a pale color of alabaster green.

I haven't been here in a while and the rush of panic nearly floors me. Luckily, before going in, I have enough wherewithal to know that I need to protect myself.

"What are you doing?" Libby runs after me when I head to the kitchen.

I grab the first knife I see, but it's short and stubby and isn't intimidating enough. I reach for a big steak knife that I haven't used once since I got the set.

Holding it firmly in front of me, I yell out, "Who's there? I'm going to call the police!"

Libby and I exchange glances. "What if it is *the police*?" she whispers.

"How could it be? You mean they left one behind?" I whisper back.

She shrugs, but she has put the doubt in my mind.

What if they placed someone here to spy on us?

Can they even do that? It wouldn't be legal, but of course, it's possible.

I walk into the guest room, adjusting the grip on the knife, trying to figure out if I should hold it with the blade down, or up, and knowing that one way is the wrong way, but not knowing which that is.

"Get behind me," I tell Libby, which is pretty unnecessary because she's already about ten feet out, lingering in the hallway.

Suddenly, I become clearly aware of the fact that there's only one way in and one way out of this room. There's a window, but I've never opened it. It's a modern, double pane window with a complicated lock and a thick screen on the other side. If this guy decides to run, his only way out is to barrel through us.

I walk into the room, look at the queen-size bed and the upholstered headboard, which took me forever to put together and connect to the frame. No one has slept here once since I bought this house, but occasionally I come here to do work because the window looks out to the front yard with a big willow tree and I like looking at it in the dead of summer.

"Who are you? What are you doing here?" I yell, flipping on the light, but I don't see anyone.

Was Libby mistaken?

Did she think that she thought she heard something, or did the guy escape while I was grabbing the knife in the kitchen?

"I heard someone right there," she says over my shoulder. "He cleared his throat."

"Are you sure?"

"Absolutely. No, he's right here. He has to be."

"He might've snuck out while we went back for the knife," I say.

She walks over to the closet and slides open the door and lets out a yelp that almost pierces my eardrum.

"What are you doing here?" I whisper, dropping the knife and covering my mouth with my hand.

"I'm sorry, I had to see you."

Tyler runs over and throws his arms over my shoulders, pressing me tightly to him. The world melts away and it's just the two of us, spinning. I hold him for as long as possible, unwilling or perhaps uncertain of whether any of this is really happening or if it's just a dream. When he pulls away, he grabs onto my shoulders and presses his lips to mine.

"It's you, it's you, I can't believe that it's you," I mumble and kiss him back over and over again.

"Why are you here? How?" I start to ask, but then I just kiss him again.

And then somewhere in the distance, I hear her clear her throat. "Oh, yeah… Libby. I'm sorry. Tyler, this is Libby. Libby, Tyler."

He pulls away from me but holds my hand tightly, intertwining his fingers with mine and extending his other hand forward.

"Wow, it's a pleasure to finally meet you," she says, cocking her head and smiling at the corner of her lips. "Glad that she didn't stab you, but you really gave us a scare."

"Yeah, I'm sorry about that." Tyler laughs.

He looks tired, worn out. His clothes hang off his body, wrinkled and full of a little bit of a musty smell.

"How did you get here?" I ask.

Libby takes a few steps back out of the doorway and I nudge him to follow her to the living room.

"What about the cops?" he asks under his breath.

"They're gone, I promise."

He shakes his head. "I saw them rush in. They were waiting outside."

"Yeah, apparently they're following me."

"Not good," he mumbles.

"You shouldn't be here," I say, my eyes meeting his. "It's not safe."

"I had to see you," he whispers back, kissing the tip of my nose and then sliding his hand over my stomach. "You're here, our baby's here."

Tyler cradles my stomach lovingly, even though there isn't much there yet in terms of mass.

"They're probably still outside," Libby says, walking over to the door and closing the upper lock. "They won't be able to get a warrant for anything, right?"

The question is directed to me, but I don’t know if she’s just asking me.

"Can I get you something to eat?" I ask, pulling away from him, but he follows closely behind, holding on to just the tips of my fingers.

"Yes, please.” Tyler nods, and I open the fridge to see what we have.

"Listen, I'm going to go," Libby says. "You two need some time alone, but it was a pleasure to meet you."

Tyler smiles and licks his lower lip.

"I'm going to throw that phone away," she tells me. "And I should probably take yours as well."

He hesitates.

"She called your number using the burner phone. If they trace that, they'll know you're here."

"I don't know if they can," he says. "What do you think?"

"I think I'm going to try to get us two whole new phones tomorrow." I nod. "Now that you're here and I know what your number will be, let's not risk it."

He hands Libby his phone, and I ask her where she's going to take them.

"Throw them in some garbage can outside of someone's house," she suggests.

I shake my head no. "What if the cops follow you? They'll be able to find them right away."

"Okay, well, I'm all out of ideas and I've got to get home."

"What if you buried them?" Tyler asks. "Not in your yard, but somewhere else, two different places. Just take out the SIM cards and bury them in two different places as well."

"You think you can do that?" I ask.

"Sure."

"Just make sure no one is following you. This is a felony. I don't know that for sure, but I'm pretty certain."

"I know, and I owe you big time."

Libby smiles again. "Just be happy, okay? That's all the thanks I need." She gives me a warm hug, tosses both phones in her purse, and walks out.

As she drives away, I watch the cops outside the house and they don't follow her.

"Good, maybe this will work," I whisper to myself.

23

ISABELLE

After Libby leaves, Tyler gives me a soft kiss and drapes his body over my shoulders, watching as I stir his omelet in the pan. He kisses my neck and plays with my hair and tells me that I'm the most beautiful woman in the world, and for once I believe him.

"This isn't safe," I say, shaking my head. "If the cops burst in and find you, they will make up anything to get their probable cause."

"I know." He nods. "But we can't leave, they're right outside. They'll follow you."

"I'm just so afraid of losing you again," I whisper.

"I'm here now," Tyler says, his eyes twinkling in the low light.

Once the eggs are ready, I top them with a little bit of cilantro and he inhales the intoxicating smell of fried onions and sits down at my kitchen table. I sit right next to him, nursing another mug of tea.

"You're not hungry?" he asks. I shake my head no. "I'll eat fast then."

"No, take your time. When was the last time you had something?"

"I can't remember. I was driving for too long."

I have so much to ask him and to talk about, but somehow the words don't come out. I just stay here in this moment with him. I watch him take big bites of my food holding my hand as if, at any moment, he's in danger of losing me again.

The fear is real. The cops are right outside, and if they knew, if anyone knew that he was here, that would be it. He'd be back in prison and I'd never see him again.

"Why did you come here?" I whisper.

"I missed you and I had nothing left in Seattle."

"What do you mean?"

"They knew who I was. They blackmailed me. It's over."

I ask for more details and he fills me in. My mouth drops open as I listen, but I'm only half-surprised.

"You lost everything," I say, watching the way that his index finger rubs the back of my palm.

"No, that was all money and things. I gained everything here with you. You and our baby are the only things that matter."

"I love you," I whisper.

"I love you, too."

Tyler reaches over, puts his hand behind my neck and pulls me closer to him, burying his fingers in my hair. I kiss him as hard as I can and shivers run down my spine as he tugs a little and presses himself firmly against me.

"I need to take a shower," he mumbles through the kiss, gets up, lifts me up with one quick motion, and walks back to the main bedroom and into my big bathroom.

We continue to kiss as I reach into the shower and turn it on. He starts to undress me and I tug at his shirt and unbuckle his pants, letting them drop to the floor.

I have a big tub right next to the walk-in shower, so he sits down on the edge and pulls me onto his lap. My legs wrap tightly around him. His body is hard and warm. When I open my eyes briefly, I see the way that his muscles flex and relax with each small movement.

I run my fingers up his biceps and down the back of his arms, feeling the strength underneath my fingertips. I make my way over to his back and feel the strength of his wingspan as he continues to kiss me over and over again.

"It should be warm now," I say when the steam starts to billow out of the top of the shower.

As soon as I step inside, the water washes over me, drenching me, and for a moment, I can't feel his hands all over my curves. As the prickles of the water collide with my skin, his mouth leaves mine for a moment and makes its way up to my ear, licking softly on my earlobe and then down my neck.

I kiss the top of his head and then bury my fingers in his hair as he makes his way down my body. He finds my nipples and cups my breasts. My core starts to feel on the verge of an explosion and I adjust my stance.

Tyler sets me down on the little step and opens my thighs and kisses me all the way down to my belly button and beyond. He takes his time, teasing me, playing with my thighs, before his fingers find their way inside, and his tongue builds that urgency within me that pushes me nearly to the edge.

But he knows my body and he knows the way that I start to tremble and he slows down his movements and pulls away just in time, giving me a wink and telling me that we're not there yet.

He pulls away briefly, cupping his hand and pouring some shampoo into it, lathering up his hair and then mine. Soap runs down my body and he flips me around and leans me against the wall. He opens my legs wide and pushes himself inside and I press my nipples to the cool wall and everything gets a little blurry and far away.

It's like everything fades except for the two of us. Quickly, our movements become a dance, a waltz. I know where to go and so does he and we start to move as one.

With him piercing through me and pushing me against the wall and with all the buildup and all the lust that I have felt for him that has gone unrequited for all of this time, it doesn't take long.

The orgasm comes in waves. It rushes through me, originating in my core and spreading all around, like a series of small earthquakes. Tyler holds me tightly as I begin to tremble, and then he starts to move faster and faster in and out of me until that same series of quakes rushes through him.

"I love you," he mumbles into my ear over the heat and the wetness and the falling water.

"I love you, too!" I yell back, loud enough to hear myself over everything.

After we dry off and wrap ourselves in our towels, I cuddle up in my silk bathrobe and hand him an old pink terrycloth one, which I haven't used in years.

He laughs, but is a good sport about it, putting it on and modeling it for me.

"I missed you," Tyler says, pulling me close to him. I inhale the pear scent that the soap has deposited on his skin. Smiling, I hug him tightly, never wanting to let go.

"I missed you, too," I whisper and we kiss again.

He leans me against the counter and reaches down to untie the belt of the robe.

"No, no, no," I say. "Not now."

"Why not? Come on, I'll be quick," he pleads, kissing my neck. He's joking, right?

"We have to talk. This is dangerous. You shouldn't be here. The cops are right outside and I'm just afraid that if we make one wrong move, that's it."

"I know." Tyler nods, taking a step away, looking down. Sitting down on the edge of the bathtub, he looks up at me. "You don't think I know that? You don't think that's something that I think about *all* the time? Everybody is looking for me. I'm a convicted felon. And once they find me, they'll throw me into that cell and they'll never let me see the light of day. That's why I need *this*."

"What?" I ask.

He reaches over and takes my hand. Slowly he intertwines his fingers with mine. "I need you with me. I need these moments between us, because I don't have anything else."

"Of course, you do."

"No, you don't understand. They're going to find me. And then we'll never be together."

"Don't say that." I snap my finger in his face. This takes him by surprise. And he leans back. "Don't you ever say that. That's not true. They won't find you unless *you* stop fighting. We can't give up. There's hope."

"What kind of hope?" Tyler shrugs. "Who's going to believe anything I say? There's no proof."

"Mallory Deals thinks there is. Mallory Deals thinks that there's DNA evidence of what really happened."

"You may think that, but he's not the prosecution and he's not the cops and he's not the judge."

"Yeah, but he's one person. And then we get a little bit more evidence and we convince another person and another person. And after a while, it becomes enough. After a while, people start to believe that you're innocent. But in order for that to happen, one thing has to happen first."

I stare deep into his eyes. He furrows his brows and then relaxes. Grabbing his chin, I force him to look up at me after looking away and asks, "What? What has to happen?"

"You." I point my finger at his chest and press it to his skin. "You have to believe. You have to believe that it's possible for us to have a life together, for us to raise this child together. And if you don't believe it, no one else will."

After getting dressed, we sit down on the edge of the bed and he asks me about my plan. I know that he doesn't have one, but that doesn't mean that I don't.

"I want to call Mallory Deals," I say. "He helped me when they took me into custody. He was there for me. He showed up on short notice."

"You think we can trust him?"

"He can be your attorney. You'd have to keep everything you say secret."

"He can't protect me," Tyler says.

"You'll have to reach out to the cops and tell them that he's with me. Otherwise, he'd be protecting a fugitive and that's a crime. He might lose his license."

"Okay."

"Why don't I call him? I don't know how to do this without him. He's the one on the outside. He is someone that can help us. Libby has her husband. The cops are outside my door. I can't just drive you somewhere. And then what? We still need help. We still need someone to work for us, to help us investigate, to find out the truth."

He shrugs. I know that he needs me to rally for him, to support him. But I need him to give back at least something. Otherwise, I don't know what's going to happen. My stomach grumbles and I start to feel sick. The day has been long and I need a nap.

"Are you okay?" Tyler asks.

I sit back against the bed, leaning on the pillow and pull out my phone.

"I'm going to call him. The cops know that he's my attorney. So they won't be able to have access to this conversation."

"Fine. If you think it's a good idea," Tyler says, reaching over and softly rubbing my feet.

I hate how defeated he is, how lost. It makes me sad because I need him to fight. But maybe he just needs to meet Mallory. Maybe that will be enough of a push to convince him that this is actually possible.

Mallory agrees to come over and, taking every precaution, I tell him about the cops out front and he promises to be careful and to tell no one.

After I hang up, we sit and wait.

"You think that I just turned you in, don't you?" I ask, leaning back on the headboard and lying down.

He lies down next to me, flips his body on his side and looks at me.

"No, I don't think so. But the less people that know about me, the better."

"How do you imagine this happening without proving your innocence? You already tried to run away."

"Come with me," he says.

"How? How do I come with you? I have to go the doctor. I have to have this baby. And the cops are on my trail. They know that if we haven't been in touch yet, we will be soon."

"Are you sure that Mallory won't tell them?" he asks after a long pause. The doorbell rings.

"Yes." I nod. "Wait here."

When I greet Mallory on the doorstep, he waves goodbye to the cops in that arrogant, confident manner that attorneys on television use.

The rain has been falling down sideways and Mallory's umbrella is soaked, but his hair is always slightly damp. He's dressed in a suit, a tie, and a trench coat, carrying a satchel bag over his shoulder.

"Thanks for coming on such short notice."

"I'm glad that you didn't tell me anything about him earlier," he says.

"Of course."

I had mentioned that Tyler was here somewhat in code, without mentioning his name, and by the eager expression on his face I can tell that Mallory is excited to finally meet the star of his online life.

I knock on the door, half expecting Tyler to not be here. There's a sliding door heading to the backyard and he could have easily slipped away. It's probably the way he had come in.

But when we enter, we see him sitting on the bench at the edge of the bed.

"Thanks for coming," he says, standing up and shaking Mallory's hand.

Mallory looks him up and down.

Jeans, flannel shirt, and hair still damp from the shower. Tyler had changed out of his bathrobe to look more professional, but in truth, he looks like he has traveled and driven for days without taking a break.

I pull all of the blinds closed. The room looks out onto the backyard that's enclosed with no cops anywhere, but I do this just in case anyone is looking over the hedges or prying from somewhere high above.

I have a desk in one corner and they bring chairs for all of us to sit around it. I offer the guys something to drink and eat, but they both settle for water.

After a long pause, Mallory pulls out a thick Manila folder and a laptop from his bag and puts it on the table.

"What's all that?" Tyler asks.

"Evidence, research into your case."

Tyler nods.

"Have you listened to my podcast?"

He shakes his head no.

Mallory is surprised. "I believe you," he says. "I believe that they may have DNA evidence proving that you're innocent."

"How so?" Tyler asks.

"Because the cops who are involved in your case are known to be crooked. There's no official evidence, but there are lots of rumors. They've had long careers and they've established certain reputations."

"Why would they frame me?" Tyler asks.

"That I do not know. There's a lot that I don't know. Why haven't you listened to my podcast?" The question is accusatory and he leans across the table and peers into Tyler's face.

I can tell that Tyler's getting angry, but he keeps his footing on the ground and his face stoic.

"Thank you for believing in my case and for following it. But I know what happened. I know that I wasn't there and I didn't want to relive it with your assumptions and contradictions and deal with all the lies that they told about me."

"You know, Isabelle told me that you can be kind of difficult. Most people would be excited to find an attorney who believed in them and did all this pro bono work on their behalf."

"Why did you do that?" Tyler asks. "I mean, didn't you have anything else to work on?"

"Proving people innocent is kind of a hobby of mine. There are a lot of felons sitting behind bars for crimes they didn't commit, but in cases like yours, they're particularly interesting."

"Why is that?" Tyler asks.

"Because it seems so black and white and clear cut. And yet when you look right below the surface, things don't make sense. But it's easier for the jury and the prosecution to create this other storyline in which everything makes sense and all the loose ends are accounted for. But you have an alibi for that night, don't you?"

Tyler nods. "Somebody I used to do more business with, but she's involved with a Mexican cartel."

"Yeah, that's what Isabelle said."

"Things have not progressed really well in that relationship," Tyler adds. "So if you're expecting her to change her mind and testify on my behalf, you're going to be waiting a really long time."

"No, I'm not. There's going to be other evidence."

"I'm not really sure about that," Tyler says with a sigh.

"What if I were to tell you that certain things are in play, certain pieces are going to be falling into place?"

"What are they?" I ask.

"I can't share now. Not until it's final… in print," he adds.

I furrow my brow.

What the hell does that mean? I wonder, but he doesn't explain.

24

TYLER

When Mallory leans back in his chair, opens the Manila folder, and starts to go over the case and everything that has happened, my mind immediately flashes back to the courtroom.

I see their exhibits blown up and shown to the jury. I watch my lawyer make a desperate plea to save my life and plead my innocence, and I remember the disgusted look on the jurors' faces when they saw the bodies of my wife and her lover.

Of course, I came home and found them there. I had to do it. There were no ifs, ands, or buts about it. I was angry. I was upset with her. I was pissed off with my partner. That's what they all assumed, but none of that was true.

What is true? Sarah and I had a complicated relationship. We lied to each other a lot, but we were also honest about who we were. I looked the other way when I saw her glancing at Greg, and maybe I shouldn't have, but I didn't really care.

The jurors didn't understand that. They wanted proof, evidence, fingerprints, everything that anyone who watches television wants.

How could a crime not have evidence, right? That is one way of thinking about it.

I've listened to Mallory's talk, presentation, or whatever you want to call it, and I want to give him a chance to help me, mostly because I don't have a choice. Isabelle thinks it's a good idea, and I want to help her to be here for her as much as I can.

She's right about one thing. If I run away, it solves nothing, but if I stay, I risk them finding me and sending me back to prison.

Mallory seems to have a solution. He knows something that he's not sharing quite yet. Something about the cops, perhaps, and everything they have covered up. None of this is news to me, but just because I know the truth, it doesn't mean that I can prove a thing.

"You should come stay with me," Mallory suggests. “It's not safe for you here with Isabelle. They’re right out there, watching her every move.”

I'm actually surprised.

"Don't look at me like that," he adds. "I told you that I believe in this case."

"I know. I'm just ... You'd be harboring a fugitive."

"Yes. I'm aware of the legal implications of what I'm doing," he says. "And no one has to know. I have a guest house. Just climb into the back seat, and we'll drive over. They'd have no reasonable reason to track me or suspect me of anything."

"Well, you are *her* attorney."

"Yes, but I have certain provisions protecting me, given the fact that I am her attorney."

I'm not really in favor of this plan, but I don't have much choice. I don't want to stay here and endanger Isabelle, the mother of my future child.

What happens if they find me here?

What happens if they find out and confirm the fact that she's been helping me?

Nothing good. That's what. They'll prosecute her. They'll try to get her to talk, and if she doesn't, they'll make it worse.

After a brief goodbye and a promise for Mallory to get us two phones, untraceable, of course, so that we can stay in touch, I head out into the backyard, hop the fence to the neighbor's property, and make my way a few streets over where Mallory picks me up. I kneel in the back just to be safe.

"I still don't understand why you're doing this," I say when we pull up next to his house.

He doesn't live too far, in a very expensive subdivision with wide lawns and houses with columns out front. He parks in the garage, closes the door, and then shows me to the backyard.

"I already told you why I'm doing this. If you don't believe me, that's your problem," Mallory says.

I nod my head, still unwilling to fully accept the answer. I have seen those podcasts out there and all of those YouTube channels devoted to true crime. I know that there is a lot of interest in these kinds of stories, and there are journalists and investigators that like to tell them. Mallory is one of them.

In the guest house, I find my whole case laid out and taped up to the walls. There's a whiteboard in the corner and a push pin board with the timeline of what happened when and what evidence was found where. Photocopies from exhibits in my case are tacked up, and I'm startled by what I see.

"Sorry. I didn't think you would be visiting. This is my workspace. It's where I record the show."

"Yeah, I see that." I nod, looking all around and running my finger over the tacks.

There are a few pictures of my wife and Greg, and I can't bring myself to look at them. There's too much blood, too much pain, and too many regrets tied up all in one picture.

I hate the fact that this is how I will remember Sarah for the rest of my life. The memories of the woman I married and the good times that we had all those years ago are starting to disappear with each passing year.

Instead, all I remember is *that.* I remember every detail of that day, where I was and what I did and can't remember years that we had spent together laughing and having fun. There has to be something wrong with that, right?

But that's what happens when there's trauma; everything stops in time. It's like there's a big pause button and you press it, and that's it. The world stops spinning.

I've tried to run away from this. I've tried to start my life over, but it keeps haunting me. If I don't at least give it an honest effort and try to make things right, try to prove my innocence and try at least as hard as a complete stranger like Mallory Deals, then what example am I setting for my unborn child?

What am I telling him or her?

That it's okay for someone to say all of these untrue things about you?

That it's okay to not fight for yourself and your family?

"I have fresh sheets right over there," Mallory says, pointing to a cupboard near the bathroom. "I'm sure you need to get some rest. I'll be here in the morning and we can talk about the plan of action."

He walks over to the door, and right before he closes it, I say, "Mallory."

He turns around.

"Thank you."

He nods.

"No, I mean it. Thank you for believing in me. Thank you for doing all of this research and putting it all out there. Thank you for helping me now."

"You're welcome. Get some rest." He smiles and walks out.

I sleep like a log. I wake up the following morning, well-rested and just briefly confused about where I am. I look around a well-designed guest house, a studio with a small kitchen, a queen-size bed, and a big desk with all of Mallory's recording equipment and research files strewn all around.

I am his subject, and his whole show is about me. I don't know exactly what led him to work on this, but when I had looked him up before, I noticed that he had done a lot of work on the Pennsylvania Innocence Project, a pro bono organization where lawyers help wrongfully convicted felons clear their sentences.

I'm glad I slept here, as my night would not have been as restful had I rented a motel room somewhere in the seedy part of town. I pull open the blinds and look outside at a little bird prancing on a twig. Somewhere in the distance I hear one sing, and I watch as a snail slowly makes her way across the grass.

In the morning, Mallory shows up. He knocks on the door carrying two cups of coffee and hands me a disposable smart phone.

"I just picked this up," he says. "I'll give Isabelle hers later today, that way you two can stay in touch."

“Thank you. This is more than generous,” I say.

“Don’t worry about it.”

”You realize, of course, that you're putting your license in danger if they find out you’re protecting me."

"Yeah, yeah, yeah.” He waves his hand in my direction. "Let me worry about that.”

We start to go over the case again. The ultimate goal is to find out who killed Sarah and Greg, but I'm not sure that information is found in the paperwork before me.

"What do you think happened, really?" Mallory asks. "What was Greg like? Was he shady? Could you trust him?"

"Like I said before, we had a major falling out because he would lie about different things and try to skim off the top from clients before paying back their profits. I didn't like this practice. They were trusting us with their money, and that was illegal and immoral, but he didn't see it that way. He thought that if they made profits and the profit was a lot higher than we had at first proposed, then what's the harm in taking an extra half a percent or so?"

"So what happened with that?" Mallory asks.

"I already told you we had a big fight, but it was unresolved. I had no idea that he was having an affair with Sarah at that time. I've already answered all of these questions. You know as much as I do. Almost everything is in the trial transcripts anyway, and no one believed me."

"I know, but you know that I have to review all the evidence, right? There are gaps and I have to find them. What are we missing here?"

I shrug my shoulders.

"There's DNA evidence that the cops didn't test," Mallory says, staring into space.

He sits across from me at the desk, gets up, and walks out of the sliding glass door. Cold wind rushes into the room, and I have no intention of following him.

Seconds later, he returns.

"Sorry about that. I thought it would be warmer outside and we'd have a little bit more space to talk."

"No problem," I mumble.

This is a studio and there's not much space to spread out. I sit on the bed, leaning against the headboard, watching Mallory pace from one side of the room to the other.

He has a very large house not too far, right across the way, but he doesn't invite me in. I don't press him. I don't even inquire about it. There must be a reason why we can't talk there. "Yeah, I think that the DNA evidence exists. The cops either framed me for this, or they're very incompetent, and I tend to think that it's the former."

"Why?" Mallory wonders out loud. "Why would they frame you?"

“I don’t know.”

He rushes over to the Manila folders and starts to go through the files one by one.

"Ryan Ashland and Brandon McPhee. That's right."

"What?" I ask.

"Those were the two detectives who worked on the case. What do you know about them?"

"Not much."

"I know something," he says. I raise my eyebrow. "They have a number of disciplinary actions on the records. All rumors, of course. Nothing official, but they're there."

"If it’s not official, how is it on their records?"

"I meant I have statements from people about their actions. Their official records, I don't know how that goes. It's all up to Internal Affairs. I think they make a note of things, but they don't type it up and sign, if you know what I mean."

I nod. This conversation is going nowhere.

I finish the last of my coffee and ask, "Are you married?" He looks up at me, surprised. "Just wanted to know a little bit about you since you know about the worst thing that has ever happened to me."

"I was." Mallory nods.

He runs his hand through his hair and clears his throat as if it's uncomfortable to talk about.

"Divorced?" I ask.

He shakes his head no. "She died four years ago."

"Oh, I'm sorry." I'm about to ask what happened when he simply says, "Breast cancer," and then shuts down.

"Have you dated anyone since?" I ask after a few moments.

"No one significant." He clears his throat and sits back down at the table to look through the paperwork.

"Why not?" I press.

"We had been together since I was twenty. I never wanted anyone else. She got everything about me. She got my jokes. I don't make that many, but she understood the ones that I did. She knew what made me tick. She knew why I do the work that I do. And how does that saying go? Once you've had the best, who needs the rest?"

"Betty White, right?" I smile.

He nods.

"What about kids?" I ask.

Mallory shrugs. "Selma and I didn't really want kids, and then she got cancer and it went into remission on and off. It was just never a good time. And now, I don't know. I don't want to bring someone into the world whose mom I don't absolutely adore, love, and I'm just not sure if I'll have that again."

I nod.

"The truth is that my dog and cat and my work, they're enough for me. They keep me entertained, and cases like yours, that's my way of giving back to the world."

Neither of us says anything for a while and I know exactly what he means. I pick up my phone and start to play around. I enter an old dummy Facebook account that I used a long time ago to catch up on friends and Isabelle.

"Wait, look at this!" Mallory exclaims. He brings the iPad over to me, his hands trembling.

I read the headline: *Detectives indicted on charges related to murder and torture.*

I read the first line of the story. "Two detectives with over forty years of combined experience were arrested Tuesday on charges related to accusations that they tortured, abused, and murdered suspects for years, going back to 2010."

"What does this mean?" I ask.

Mallory's eyes light up.

"Who are they talking about?"

He scrolls down and points to the names of the detectives who testified against me in court and three others.

"I had a Google alert set up on their names and it finally pinged!"

I zoom in on the picture of Ryan Ashland with his hands in handcuffs and his head down, shoulders slouching, walking toward the courthouse next to his partner, Brandon McPhee. They are both escorted by officers.

"Must've done something really bad to get perpetrator walk pictures like this," Mallory says. "That's something that cops only do to suspects they really don't like, and it's not usually reserved for anyone who turned himself in, let alone two decorated officers."

"What do you think this means?" I ask.

My head starts to feel fuzzy. A part of me is excited, but I almost don't want to let myself believe that this is happening.

"This means we have leverage." Mallory smiles at me.

"What kind of leverage?"

"I don't know exactly, but if you think that there's DNA evidence and they're arrested for doing something this bad and there are pictures of them walking into the courtroom like *this*, the detectives on the force are mad as hell.

They're going down, and they're going to be talking."

"Okay. I need a minute," I say, getting up and walking outside.

I'm dressed in just a flannel-shirt and jeans, and the cold gusts of air keep slamming into me, but I feel nothing. I'm not exactly vindicated. Far from it, but suddenly there's a sliver of hope.

It's like when the sky is full of clouds, and then something changes and a little ray of light shines through, and it reminds you that, hey, maybe sunshine is possible. Maybe hope is not something that's just going to be a noose around your neck to hang yourself with, but rather something you can use to get what you want.

I meander around Mallory's backyard. It's a big wide field with a basketball court to one side, backing onto a thick wooded area. It's probably not safe for me to be out here, but the crisp air feels good in my lungs, and I need to give myself time to breathe.

The article in the Pittsburgh Post-Gazette is followed up by a few others, basically containing the same information from the press release. I read each one to make sure that it's the same Ryan Ashland and Brandon McPhee who had arrested and testified against me all those years ago. They are bigger now, chubbier, and one has a thick receding hairline. The day you get arrested is not the best time for a photo shoot, but they look particularly haggard and beaten down.

Unable to find any particularly in-depth, juicy gossip in print, I go to Twitter and put in their names to see what people are saying. Most of the comments mention corruption going back years.

At least four people write stories about friends and family members who have been arrested and framed with drugs or weapons to trump up their charges and to give them long sentences. No one writes anything in support of them or their collaborators.

A few minutes later, when the cold doesn't just nip at my fingers but starts to penetrate deep inside my core, I finally go back inside and find Mallory waving something in my face.

"It's Isabelle," Mallory says, handing me the phone.

"Hey, what's going on?" I ask, holding the strange phone up to my face. Isabelle has a concerned look on her face.

"He told me what happened. The cops were arrested."

"Yeah, they were."

"What does this mean?" she asks. I look at her face on the screen and let out a little sigh.

My breathing is getting easier. The boulder that has been sitting on my chest this whole time actually has a possibility of being removed.

"Mallory is going to look into it. He thinks that there's a lot of evidence that they're pretty crooked in addition to this case and maybe one of them will be willing to talk about what happened."

"But why, why would they do that?" Isabelle asks.

"What do you mean?"

"Well, they will just be implicating themselves in more cases if they say anything about yours."

Mallory steps back into the frame.

"There're a lot of ways that these deals are done. If one or two collaborate and cooperate and tell the investigators about something on the others, they'll get a lower sentence. And if they bring in extra evidence from other cases, like Tyler's, that could go a long way in helping things as well."

Isabelle smiles at the corner of her mouth. Her eyes look tired, but I tell her that she's beautiful. Mallory steps away and says that he has something to get in the main house, leaving us alone.

"How are you?" I ask.

"I'm okay, just feeling really sick this morning."

"Throwing up?"

She nods.

"I can't wait to see the baby."

"I went to the doctor today," she says, moving her hair from side to side. She pulls out a small gray, black, and white picture with a little triangle in the center.

"Is that it? That's the ultrasound?"

She nods, holding it up to the screen. "That's your little boy," she says. And it feels like the world has stopped spinning on its axis.

"We're having a little boy?"

She nods, grinning from ear to ear.

"Really?"

"Really, really." She laughs.

She waits while I take a screenshot and then puts the phone next to her face.

"We have to make this work," I say. "I have to get this case overturned."

"Yes, we do." She nods.

"I want to be there for the birth. I want to be there for all of the doctors' appointments, even right now just to hold up your hair while you puke."

"Wow, that's very romantic but I think I'm fine without you being there in the bathroom with me."

I laugh and so does she and for a second, it feels just like it should; a couple in love expecting their first child.

"I want you to marry me," I say.

Her eyes snap up to mine. "What are you talking about? What are you doing?"

"I know that I should be on my knees with a ring, but everything else in our relationship has been so complicated and bizarre but I want you to marry me as soon as we can and not just because of the baby, but because when you realize that you want to spend the rest of your life with someone, you want that to happen as soon as possible."

A tear rolls down her cheek. She inhales slowly and her nose is congested just a little bit.

"What do you say?" I ask.

"Yes," she mumbles, holding back more tears. "Of course, of course I want to marry you."

"Okay. I love you."

She nods and says that she has to go. "I'm sorry, I just don't feel very good right now, but I'll call back later."

"Okay." I hang up and put Mallory's phone on the counter.

I stare at the screen and wonder how all of this is going to transpire and work out and if good and right things have truly ever worked out in real life.

25

ISABELLE

My contractions start when I'm with a client in Allison Park. I was supposed to stop working a week ago, but Everett's parents are splitting up, and due to the stress, he had a big delay in his speech. I'm not sure if I'll be able to meet with him again for at least two more months so I don't want to miss this appointment.

I'm feeling fine when I arrive, and my due date is still two days away, but in the middle of our session, I start to feel the contractions. The pain is startling.

It grabs ahold of me and I can't breathe as the wave rushes through me. I excuse myself and Everett continues to play with trains on the floor, pointing and shouting and using the new word, "rocket," that he had just learned.

In the middle of the fourth contraction, he finally notices.

"Okay?" he asks, slurring the word.

"Yes, I'm fine," I whisper, grabbing onto the table to steady myself.

I focus my thoughts and try to remember what I learned when I did the meditation exercises online, but my mind goes blank. The pain just pulses through me, and I count slowly until it passes.

I look at my watch. They are ten minutes apart.

Okay, I am supposed to go to the hospital when I'm five minutes apart, so I have time. This takes a while. I end up pushing through the rest of the session.

"Do you want me to drive you to the hospital?" Everett's mom asks. "Call someone?"

"No, it's okay. I'll get there." I call Tyler on the way, and he tells me that he'll meet me straight there. I call Libby as well, and she promises to come even though I tell her not to. I'm still a long way out, and who knows how long labor will take.

"Don't worry about it," she says. "I'll be there."

As I drive to the hospital, one of my contractions happens when I'm parked at a stoplight, and I let it pass over me before stepping on the accelerator. It's probably not the safest thing in the world to drive in this state, but I'm a good half an hour away, and I don't have much choice.

An ambulance would be way too expensive, and this delivery will probably be over thirty grand and who knows how much the insurance will cover. Tyler keeps telling me not to worry about money, but I can't help it.

About five minutes away from the hospital, a really bad contraction comes on and I slam on the brakes. Luckily, I'm going down a relatively empty street with no one behind me.

I ride the wave as I stand double-parked next to an old Victorian house, and I take my mind elsewhere to try to forget the pain. The last eight months have been a challenge to say the least, but there has been a lot of lucky things that have happened that have really turned the tide in our direction.

The detectives who were arrested were not only crooked and corrupt, but they were also indicted and convicted of a series of murders for taking suspects and torturing them for information in various black spots around the city, eventually killing three. All five of them cooperated with the authorities. There was a lot of evidence, but in order to get better deals, each one told what they knew and more. With each confession, investigators got more and more of the story.

That's how we found out that there was DNA evidence that was collected at the scene but never tested, and that this was not an oversight.

Ashland and McPhee never tested the evidence because they already knew who it belonged to. They even tried to destroy it, but they couldn't find the files when the lab moved to another building. McPhee admitted this in his confession when he cooperated in order to get a lighter sentence. When it was finally located, McPhee hairs were found at the scene.

I remember what McPhee looked like when he told the story in court, confident and arrogant and hardly sorry for what they did.

His reasoning? Apparently they had both lost money in a fund that Greg and Tyler had managed. They thought that Tyler had stolen it, and they wanted to make both of them pay for what happened. They found out about the affair that Greg was having with Tyler's wife and decided to kill him, his wife, and frame Tyler for the murders.

In order to refute his partner's story and put the blame squarely on his shoulders, McPhee got on the stand and went over basically the same gist, making a few changes here and there to protect himself. By the time they'd both testified, I was still not certain as to which one of them came up with the idea and which one of them shot whom, but one thing was for sure, they were the ones who did it, not Tyler.

I manage to park the car and walk into the hospital on my own before another contraction pulls me down onto the floor. Somebody runs up to me and helps me into a wheelchair. When the pain slows down and abates just a little bit, I tell them my name and they roll me into a room where Tyler is waiting.

"How are you? Are you okay?" he asks, his body is tense and flushed, and his face is covered in worry lines.

"I'm fine." I wave my hand at him. "I just need something to drink. My mouth is so dry."

"Yes, of course."

He reaches over to his bag and hands me a flask of water. I get up from the wheelchair and sit down on the edge of the bed.

"I brought your bag," he says. "It's all packed. If you need anything else, I can just run back home."

"Yeah, that's great." I nod, starting to feel like another contraction is about to come on, but it doesn't.

I grab his hand and intertwine mine with his. I bring it to my lips and give him a kiss. His wedding ring glistens under the harsh fluorescent lights, and I run my fingers over it, feeling its smooth titanium finish.

"I'm so glad we did this," I say, twisting it around his finger.

"Yes, me, too." He nods, giving me a kiss on the cheek.

We went to the Justice of the Peace three months ago, a day after he agreed to take the Alford plea. Whether or not to accept that plea deal was something that we went back and forth on for a while, but the State of Pennsylvania and the prosecution were adamant.

If they were to overturn his sentence, then they would be subject to a multimillion dollar lawsuit for false imprisonment. But if Tyler agreed to take the plea in which he, the defendant, would maintain his innocence but acknowledge that the government had sufficient evidence to convict, then they would drop all charges related to his escape from prison. And the thing is that even if his case were overturned as a result of what the cops had admitted to on the stand, it is still a crime to escape from prison, and they could have given him years just for that.

I wanted to fight on, but I was terrified of losing him for years. The prosecutor told Mallory that he'd have no choice but to arrest him for escape and this was the only bargaining chip we had. This was our compromise. Tyler agreed to the plea deal to gain his freedom.

Libby arrives and checks on me about an hour later. My contractions are five minutes apart now. I can still talk, but I have a hard time joking around while I wait for the next one to come on.

I'm glad that she's here because it helps me hide my fears about what I'm about to do. It's also nice to have her here because she reminds me of the fact that women have actually done this in the past and lived, a longtime fear of mine.

She stays for close to two hours chatting and trying to distract me from the pain and help Tyler. She and Tyler have become close as well, and she's glad that he doesn't hold anything against her husband for calling the cops on me. All's well that ends well, right?

Though Tyler has been incredibly lucky here, given how this whole case unfolded, he's also been incredibly unlucky in the past, and we talk about that often. It's good to take stock of your life and to appreciate what you have instead of focusing on what you don't.

Nineteen hours later, after I have played what seems to be every mobile game there is and watched hours of Netflix, my labor stops progressing. We had a talk about this five hours ago when the doctor came in and said what could happen.

At some point, a C-section would be in order, and I'm fine with that. In fact, I'm a little bit less scared of having a planned C-section than I am of actually giving birth and having possible tearing and all the other complications than I am of an emergency C-section.

The doctor comes in and makes the suggestion that we start making preparations to do the procedure.

I agree and sit up to get the shot in my back.

"We have to take you to the operating room for that," she says with a smile. "But it's all ready now, so why don't you, Tyler, get dressed in these scrubs and we'll call you over right before the procedure starts, and then you'll be able to see your little boy."

"Okay," he says, looking nervous all of a sudden. This whole time, he has been so calm and collected, but now he looks scared.

"Everything's going to be fine," Dr. Laden assures him and squeezes my hand. "It's going to be quick and painless."

"You're going to do great," Tyler whispers in my ear and gives me a kiss as they lead me to the operating room.

"I love you," he adds.

"I love you, too."

I still have my phone on me as I wait outside the door for them to finish setting up. As I scroll through social media, I get a Google Alert email. My hands begin to tremble as I click on it.

Mac Salish, suspected murderer in the killing of 23-year-old Maggie McPherson, an elementary school teacher, has been shot in a confrontation with police in Nevada City, Nevada.

I read the article over and over again, skimming it and then reviewing it in parts as I try to put the pieces together.

Maggie McPherson was an elementary school teacher who ran away from her abusive boyfriend and lived what the writer called "a transient lifestyle." She and Mac were spotted in California and then Washington traveling together but then her body was found in a Motel 6 near Las Vegas and Mac was the prime suspect in her murder. She had been stabbed to death.

Mac's body was found with a suitcase of almost sixty-thousand dollars in cash and five automatic weapons. His partner in the famous prison escape was Tyler McDermott who has had his sentence overturned.

“Isabelle, I'm going to have to take your phone," the nurse says and wheels me in.

They give me the epidural shot as I hold the pillow and think of the life that we have escaped and the one that we now get to live, thanks to what Tyler did by running away from prison.

And yet, things could have gone awry just like they did for Maggie. She didn’t deserve to die.

What was her life with Mac like and how did it come to such a tragic end? There’re so many things that I won't know the answers to and I’ll have to be okay with it. It's good to close one chapter of your life before beginning another.

I was nauseous and throwing up for my entire pregnancy and the day that I deliver is no different. As I lie down on the table and they put the curtain up in front of my face, I start to feel sick to my stomach and an anesthesiologist holds my head, directing me to throw up into some sort of basin. Tyler's behind the curtain with me, careful not to look and see me split open.

"Have you started cutting yet?" I ask and I hear laughter on the other side.

“We’ve been at it for a few minutes already.” Dr. Laden laughs.

A moment later, she holds up my baby to me and hot tears start to roll down my cheeks.

"He's here," I whisper.

"Yes, you did it." Tyler squeezes my shoulders.

"We're going to get him cleaned up and we'll bring him right back," the nurse says.

As they start to sew me up, they bring him back for a few minutes and I reach over and hold him, touch him, and make sure that he's real and he's actually mine. And then they hand him to Tyler who smiles lovingly at him and kisses me.

"We have to go and finish putting you back together," the nurse smiles, "and then we'll bring you out."

It takes a little bit over forty-five minutes for me to get stitched up and wrapped up like I'm a mummy before they roll my bed into a small room with a window and tell me that my husband and son will be here soon.

Alone with my thoughts, I contemplate the meaning of that statement.

Not long ago, I had neither and I was lost and nothing seemed to make sense in my world and now, what more could I want?

What more is there to have besides these two loves of my life?

The door swings open and Tyler walks in holding our baby in his arms, smiling from ear to ear.

He places him into my arms and I look at his squished little face and I know that my life will never be the same again.

He wants something else: **me, for one year.**

But I don't even know who he is…

365 days and nights doing everything he wants…except that.

"I'm not going to sleep with you," I say categorically.

He laughs.

"I'm going to make you a promise," his eyes challenge mine. **"Before our time is up, you'll beg me for it."**

Read TELL ME TO STOP now!

CONNECT WITH CHARLOTTE BYRD

Sign up for my **newsletter** to find out when I have new books!

You can also join my Facebook group, **Charlotte Byrd's Reader Club**, for exclusive giveaways and sneak peaks of future books.

I appreciate you sharing my books and telling your friends about them. Reviews help readers find my books! Please leave a review on your favorite site.

Sign up for my newsletter: https://www.subscribepage.com/byrdVIPList

Join my Facebook Group: https://www.facebook.com/groups/276340079439433/

Bonus Points: Follow me on BookBub and Goodreads!

ALSO BY CHARLOTTE BYRD

All books are available at ALL major retailers! If you can't find it, please email me at charlotte@charlotte-byrd.com

The Perfect Stranger Series

The Perfect Stranger

The Perfect Cover

The Perfect Lie

The Perfect Life

The Perfect Getaway

All the Lies Series

All the Lies

All the Secrets

All the Doubts

Tell me Series

Tell Me to Stop

Tell Me to Go

Tell Me to Stay

Tell Me to Run

Tell Me to Fight

Tell Me to Lie

Wedlocked Trilogy

Dangerous Engagement

Lethal Wedding

Fatal Wedding

Tangled Series

Tangled up in Ice

Tangled up in Pain

Tangled up in Lace

Tangled up in Hate

Tangled up in Love

Black Series

Black Edge

Black Rules

Black Bounds

Black Contract

Black Limit

Not into you Duet

Not into you

Still not into you

Lavish Trilogy

Lavish Lies

Lavish Betrayal

Lavish Obsession

Standalone Novels

Dressing Mr. Dalton

Debt

Offer

Unknown

ABOUT CHARLOTTE BYRD

Charlotte Byrd is the bestselling author of romantic suspense novels. She has sold over 600,000 books and has been translated into five languages.

She lives near Palm Springs, California with her husband, son, and a toy Australian Shepherd. Charlotte is addicted to books and Netflix and she loves hot weather and crystal blue water.

Write her here:

charlotte@charlotte-byrd.com

Check out her books here:

www.charlotte-byrd.com

Connect with her here:

www.facebook.com/charlottebyrdbooks

www.instagram.com/charlottebyrdbooks

www.twitter.com/byrdauthor

Sign up for my newsletter: https://www.subscribepage.com/byrdVIPList

Join my Facebook Group: https://www.facebook.com/groups/276340079439433/

Bonus Points: Follow me on BookBub and Goodreads!

facebook.com/charlottebyrdbooks
twitter.com/byrdauthor
instagram.com/charlottebyrdbooks
bookbub.com/profile/charlotte-byrd

Made in the USA
Columbia, SC
14 August 2021